ORIGINAL WITCH

DREAMSHIFTERS BOOK ONE

CAMERON DRAKE
KARA SEVDA

Contents

ALSO BY KARA SEVDA

For our families

ORIGINAL WITCH

I *just met the boy of my dreams— literally. But there's a catch. He's turning into a werewolf. And I think I might be a witch.*

In the small town where I grew up, I was a little odd, but who wasn't? I never told anyone about my dreams, where I went in them, or who I met; no one told me about *their* weird problems either.

But when I left for college, the dreams followed me… and now they're *real*.

The startlingly handsome boy I've been dreaming about for years? He's in my freshman lit class.I try to avoid him but he doesn't take the hint.

And then things start getting *really* weird.

The boy from my dreams? The one I see all over campus? Turns out he's dreamed about me, too.

I just want to be a normal college student, with a normal life and a normal boyfriend. ***But I'm not.*** Lights blow out when I'm angry. I know certain things before they happen. Butterflies follow me when I'm in a good mood.

If I'm going to save myself and the boy of my literal dreams, I need to figure out what is happening to us and why.

And I need to do it fast.

A NOTE ABOUT ORIGINAL WITCH

This book was originally released under another title. It has been completely reimagined and rewritten, though some elements of the story remain the same.

PROLOGUE

The little girl giggled, pushing backwards on her tiptoes. She kicked her legs out as she sped forward on the swing. She was waiting for the real fun to start.

Her mama was supposed to come out and push her before dinner. She couldn't get very high without someone strong behind her. They had made a habit of coming out here each night to watch the apple blossoms fall.

With each swing, the tree gave up some of its fading petals. She leaned backwards, letting the pale pink blossoms shower over her face.

She could smell them, sweet and rare and slightly rotten. Like an apple that had been left out in the sun. A bird peered down at her from the gnarled branches, chirping loudly.

Then the butterflies came.

"Mama!"

Tiny purple butterflies swirled around her as her mother came out to the yard to watch. Her mother's beautiful face was tired, almost faded. But she still smiled kindly for her daughter.

Her mother had been having bad dreams, Krista knew.

They shared a room in the tiny, sun-washed house. The yellow paint was faded to almost white, the shutters hanging on by a thread. But it was home. Three generations of the women in their family had laid their heads there, and the little girl loved the old house.

The girl tried to hide her yawn from her mother. She had played in the sun all afternoon, the birds and butterflies

3

performing acrobatics just for her. Her Grandmother sat outside with her, watching the child so her daughter could sleep.

Something was wrong, but they did their best to get along.

It was later when the little girl curled up in the tiny twin bed with her mother, her belly full and a sense of right in the world. That night her mother didn't cry out in fear. That night her mother barely stirred an inch. Not until she crept out in the pale dawn night.

In the morning, she was gone.

CHAPTER 1

DEAN

"Come on champ, one last kegger."

I stared out at the water. My friends were digging a pit for a bonfire, dragging out beach chairs and blankets and less wholesome supplies for the party.

A box full of half empty bottles of alcohol, and a garbage can full of ice for the first of many kegs.

"You can't leave man. It's our last chance to be together."

"Yeah. Okay."

I was tired. I was having trouble sleeping. The sad part was, I was desperate to fall asleep.

I just wanted to see her.

The girl with the dark hair and the sad, but hauntingly beautiful eyes.

I spent most nights staring at the ceiling, waiting for her. But if I didn't sleep, I didn't see her. I debated about sneaking one of my mom's sleeping pills.

If I did that — if I went under long enough — maybe she would come.

It had been weeks since she visited me.

"Here, have some of the good stuff before all the kiddies show up."

I accepted the cold bottle of beer from my buddy Jason and drank deep. I'd have a couple, and hope it wound me down. Just a few and then I'd go home.

I didn't care if this was the last time I would be with all my teammates and high school friends before I left for college.

I didn't care that things would never be the same again.

I only wanted one thing.

I wanted her.

CHAPTER 2

KRISTA

That night I knew I would go to him.

I slipped into the covers, knowing that I would be sleeping somewhere new soon. I looked at the old tree out the window, wishing I could bring the sight and smell of it with me.

The branches waved slightly in the wind.

Almost like they were saying goodbye.

I was excited for tomorrow, but I dreaded sleep. Dreaded it, as much as I longed to see him.

The dreams were getting worse. Each night it began the same way. I would rise from my bed and stand, still wearing my worn-in old nightgown. It was soft and threadbare from being washed more times than I could count. There was a little bit of lace around the neckline that was starting to tear.

Like me, it was perfectly ordinary and familiar for the first few moments of the dream. My bedroom looked the same, my house, my street outside the window. My long, dark hair waved behind me, moving as if it had a mind of its own.

But in my dreams, everything else was different.

I would take a step, and then another, my feet never quite touching the ground. I climbed out of the window, barely feeling the curtains as they brushed my shoulders. I would stand on the pitched roof, feeling the cool night air on my face.

And then I'd step off into nothingness.

And fly.

I did not fly like a bird. It was more like floating on air, like gliding. But that wasn't it exactly either.

It was as if I had springs in my legs and a loose tether to this world. Gravity had little sway over me. In the night, I did not bow to its rules. Each step would take me ten to twelve feet. Sometimes I would rise twenty feet or higher, fingers scraping against the streetlights.

In the dreams, I was not afraid of the strange magic of it all. It made sense to me. It did not make me feel like a freak.

It the dreams, I belonged.

And sometimes, I would blink and be in another place.

Of course, you couldn't *really* blink in dreams.

I knew that. I was a rational human being. Even in the dreams I knew that.

The world followed certain rules and you had to obey them. Red meant stop. Green meant go. Girls didn't fly or leap or travel hundreds of miles to visit a beautiful boy that made their heart flutter and their breath catch.

You didn't actually breathe in dreams. Your pulse didn't really race. You didn't fall in love.

Only that wasn't entirely true. I knew because I had felt all those things. And more.

On certain nights, I would find myself going to the same familiar house in the same sleepy town. I didn't know where it was, or what the town was called.

I knew it was near the sea, with a sandy coast and the tang of salt in the air. I'd never been there in my waking life, but I often found myself staring up at his window in my dreams.

The boy I visited. I'd never met him before in real life. He wasn't an actor or someone I'd seen on TV.

I knew because I'd tried to find him.

I had been searching for him for years. It wasn't easy with so little to go on. But every now and then, I'd go online and down the rabbit hole all the same.

Just to figure out if I was crazy.

Some nights I would blink and find myself on his roof, like some sort of cat burglar. Or more accurately, a stalker.

Yeah, I was starting to feel a little bit creepy about my nocturnal visits.

He was rich. The boy lived in a big house with large white columns, set in the middle of vast manicured lawns. I would look around for a minute or two. Then I'd be in his bedroom, staring down at him, with no idea of how I'd gotten there.

He was a restless sleeper, often tangled up in the sheets, his hair falling over his eyes.

Some nights I would reach out, my hand pressing his chest. His eyes would open and like me, he would rise from the bed.

I didn't know his name or how old he was. I didn't know if he was real. All I knew was that he was beautiful.

That the stormy dark blue of his eyes reminded me of the sea.

The sea… I'd never seen in it person. But I knew it well from the dreams. The cool sand beneath my bare feet. The salty smell. The vastness of the ocean.

The feeling that it could swallow me up and make me disappear.

The boy loved the ocean too.

We'd often go there together and watch the night sky. I would take his hand and we would be there, just like that, listening to the waves crash on a deserted beach.

He was always startled by the sudden leaps to a new location. I was used to it and could control it sometimes, though it was never an entirely conscious decision. I knew on some level that I was dreaming so I never panicked when I found myself someplace new.

I was different in the dreams.

I would never have talked to a handsome boy in real life, let alone visited him in his house uninvited. But I was sure of myself in the dreams. Confident in a way I never was when I was awake.

Or at least I was until he kissed me.

Last night had changed everything. I could still feel his hands where they had pressed my cheeks, guiding me towards him. His lips had felt so real, so hot that they almost scalded me.

The dream had stuck with me even longer than usual, the vivid memory of the kiss keeping me distracted and tense while I packed and cleaned.

Most people forgot their dreams. But I never did.

Especially not this one.

How many girls could say that their first kiss happened in a dream?

CHAPTER 3

DEAN

*H**ere we go.*

I stood in the doorway to my new room. It was spacious, with a full-sized bed, dark wood desk, and dresser. A window overlooked the woods that bordered the school.

As a member of the University football team, I was rooming on a separate part of the campus. The townhouses were reserved just for athletes. We were given special housing, just for being on the team.

Really nice housing.

Of course, I was used to really nice housing. Our family home was a two hundred-year-old mansion, even if my parents refused to call it that. The three of us rattled around the estate, hardly ever bumping into each other except for meal times.

This would be different.

For the first time in my life, I'd be living in close proximity with other people my own age. It would be loud. And messy. But hopefully less boring and lonely.

Yeah, the giant old house kind of felt like a museum. It was not really that exciting for a boy growing up. The only people under thirty in my parent's house were servants.

But here, I had roommates.

Right next door, knock on the wall if you need something, probably going to be annoying as hell roommates.

Still, I couldn't lie. I was more than a little excited to be here. For once in my life, I wouldn't be just the heir to the richest family in the state. No one knew who I was, or who my family was.

Here I was just another student. An athlete, but still. I was practically normal.

Each player was in a suite with three other teammates. We had private rooms with a central living room and a large kitchen on one side of the room. We even had our own *en suite* bathrooms, along with a half bath in the main living area.

I was aware that the rest of the student population did not live like this. Especially not the Freshman. After Sophomore year, you could move off campus, but only the richest students could afford anything like the townhouses the athletes got.

Well, not *all* the athletes.

The best housing was reserved for the football team.

It was a football school and the players were treated like kings. And I was their prize catch for the year. I'd been told I was going to get field time in almost every game, to prep me to take over as lead quarterback next year as a Sophomore.

My future was neatly mapped out for me. I was at a top tier school. I had a bright career in either sports or business ahead of me. Maybe both.

Everything was being handed to me on a silver platter.

I should be ecstatic.

But as usual, I felt like something was missing. And not something I could tell anyone else about. Nobody would understand. Even worse, they would think I was crazy.

I'd never told anyone about it. Any of it. I'd never even considered mentioning the gaping hole I felt inside me. The hole that only one, impossible thing could fill.

Her.

The girl from my dreams.

The beautiful girl with the big gray eyes that seemed to stare right through me. The touch of her hand when she woke me. She came at least once a month for the past several years. And her lips… I'd been dreaming about kissing her for years but only last week had I dared to actually do it.

And the kiss had been epic.

I had girlfriends in real life. I wasn't vain but I knew what people saw when they looked at me. A rich, tall, built guy with good looks who was by far the best athlete my hometown had seen in a decade. Girls fell into my lap with an almost annoying frequency. But I'd never been too invested in anything romantic.

Not while I was awake anyway.

On some level, I knew it wasn't fair to compare the girls from my high school to her delicate, ethereal beauty. But I couldn't help but notice these real, flesh and blood girls seemed silly and superficial next to her.

The sad-eyed beauty from my sleeping life was somehow more *real* than any of those girls could ever be. And to me, it really *was* a whole other life.

A life I wished I could escape to more often than not.

I knew that other people didn't dream like I did. Nowhere near as extensively and nowhere near as vividly. My dreams were almost brighter than real life somehow.

More substantial.

I didn't get to go there every night though. Only when she was there. She was the key to the kingdom.

"Dean? Want to help me with this buddy?"

My dad called up from the street where he was unloading the van we'd rented. Not a grubby old moving van, either. No, this one was bright white and practically brand new. Like everything in my life, it was over the top and excessive. Something I was getting tired of, if I was honest.

Nothing but the best for the Westens.

My mother had gone all out as usual. A new laptop, an easy chair with an ottoman, an ergonomic desk chair, and thousand thread count sheets with matching quilts and blankets.

There were throw pillows and a rug to 'tie it all together.' She'd even packed some artwork, tastefully framed posters of places we'd travelled over the years. Plus a few concert posters for the old rock bands that she knew I loved.

It already looked like an interior design magazine's version of a college dorm room.

I grimaced. I did not want to be labeled as a spoiled rich kid on day one. My parents had overdone it as usual. They meant well though. I decided not to say anything, knowing I could

always tone it down later.

I ran down the stairs to help unload the rest of the van. If nothing else, it would get them out of here faster. And then I could hide the damn throw pillows in the closet.

I was nothing if not a dutiful son.

CHAPTER 4

KRISTA

*E*verything was gray.

It was misty as I peered eagerly out the dirty window. This was a monumental moment. I wanted to brush the dirt away so I could see it.

The start of my new life.

The bus pulled to a stop in front of a dingy bus depot. I leaned forward, my forehead nearly pressed against the glass. It was a gray, chilly day for September, but nothing could dampen my spirits.

Or soothe the small knot of nerves in the pit of my belly. Just butterflies, Nan would say. But it felt more like a tiny tornado. Nothing sweet or pretty about it.

I pushed my nerves down. This was it. I was here at long last. My first day at college. It didn't matter that I was stiff and in sore need of a shower after eighteen hours on a smelly old bus.

Today I got to rewrite history.

I was no longer the odd girl from the edge of a tiny, backwater Louisiana town. I was not the girl whose mother had run off and abandoned me. I was not the one wearing clothes with patches and everybody else's hand-me-downs.

As of today, I could be anyone I damn well wanted to be.

It was pretty much the best day of my life.

It was the *first* day of my life.

I stood on the sidewalk with my bags at my feet, looking around. There was a grubby old coffee shop and a few low rent looking storefronts. But to me, it was all exciting.

You would think the bus would stop directly in front of the college, considering the school was the top draw for the town, but no. The University was at the edge of town, far from the gritty downtown area where the bus let out.

Well, it was a large town or a small city. I wasn't really sure which. But for the next four years, it was home.

Either way it was already way more glamorous than where I'd come from. If I had my way, I would never be going back home again. Only to visit and see Nan. Never for any longer than a quick visit. That chapter was over.

The new Krista was here.

I heaved my second-hand backpack over my shoulders. It was heavy, but thankfully a lifetime of chores had made me strong. Inside it were my prized possessions: my pillow, a couple of favorite books I read over and over again when I couldn't sleep, and a sketchpad. My primary escape vehicles.

One for reading, one for drawing, and one for dreaming.

The ancient army navy store duffle bag contained two pairs of jeans, a handful of t-shirts, two button downs, a cardigan and a jean jacket that was a little on the tight side.

Actually, *everything* was a little tight across the chest these days, what with my bosoms coming in late. That had facilitated a last-minute trip to the local thrift shop. Most of the unstained shirts happened to be in the men's section, so that's what I had. Nan had taken up the sleeves so I wasn't swimming in them. Other than my underthings and a couple of nightgowns, that was all I had brought.

It was everything I owned, more or less.

Every last bit of it was rolled up into the beautiful quilt Nan had given me for my sixteenth birthday. The quilt was painstakingly crafted of scraps from sewing projects, faded curtains and, most meaningfully, from a few of the old dresses my mother had left behind.

Those little snips and bits were all I had left of my mother. It wasn't much, but it kept me warm and safe at night. And that magical feeling stayed with me all through the night, even in my dreams.

Until I had to wake up and face the real world, anyway.

On my feet were my one pair of sneakers, my only other pair of shoes was the broken in penny loafers that swung from my arm in a plastic grocery bag. Nan had taught me to keep my shoes away from clean clothes and bedding long ago. If I got on the bed with my shoes on even once, I never heard the end of it.

'Traveling light' my grandmother called it. 'Being poor' was a more accurate way to put it. Money had always been tight, even before Mom had disappeared on us. But after, things got a lot worse.

I never went hungry though, or without clean, mended clothes to wear. So I didn't see the point in complaining.

My stomach growled at the thought of food. Speaking of which, I was in dire need of something to eat.

It was mid-morning and I was starving. I'd gotten on the bus yesterday afternoon with a bag full of snacks. Mostly fruit but also a tuna fish sandwich and one of my favorite bags of chips. Those were long gone, as was the bottled water and iced tea I'd brought along to sip.

I asked directions and started walking the half a mile from the bus station to campus. I stopped and got an iced tea from a deli and kept walking. No need to show up with a scratchy throat, but I didn't feel like eating a sandwich on the street.

I hoped the dining hall was open soon. That was included in my scholarship, so all my meals had to come from there. I knew the food wouldn't be like home cooking, but I prayed it wouldn't be too bad. Not that it would matter at the moment.

All this walking was working up an appetite

I didn't mind the long walk too much though. It was a beautiful day and I was getting a chance to get the lay of the land.

Besides, this was nothing new. I was used to being hungry now and then. Not starving. Nan set a good table. But there wasn't always enough for seconds. And snacking was a foreign concept in our house.

Like Nan always said, dirt poor wasn't just an expression.

But I made it here. I was going to college. The first in our family. All thanks to financial aid and several scholarships. Nan had always pushed me to work hard at school and it had paid off. I had earned both merit and hardship assistance. Even with that, I already owed more money than Nan's tiny house was worth. Or at least I would by the end of the year.

Never mind how deep I would be in the hole after four years… it boggled the mind to think about it. For the thousandth time, I had misgivings about what I was doing. What if I couldn't pay it back? What then, genius?

I hadn't even set foot on campus yet or learned one thing and I was already in over my head. Not just a little either.

Better make this count, girl.

I nodded to myself. I had a habit of making things count. Art class at school for one thing. Mrs. Craddock had developed a system of letting me stay after school to use all the supplies. I was her star pupil after all, and my teacher had known that money was hard to come by.

Those long afternoons practicing had earned me a spot in the coveted Fine Arts department, as well as provided the portfolio that had won me yet another scholarship in mixed media. I loved drawing, painting and sculpture, though I planned to major in Art History, and minor in fine art.

It was safer. Smarter. And lord knows I had to be smart. The cards were already stacked against me.

I was sweaty and tired by the time I set foot on campus. It was another hour before I found my dorm.

I stared up at the gray stone building. It was bigger than the courthouse back home. I squared my shoulders and climbed the three flights to my dorm room.

The hallway was bustling, with parents and kids everywhere. There were trunks and boxes and luggage clogging the way. I nudged my way through, trying to be polite about it.

I groaned as I rounded the last set of stairs, dragging my bags down the hallway behind me.

I pushed the door open to my room. It wasn't empty. I felt the air whoosh out of my lungs as I took in the sight in front of me.

A pretty blonde girl was already arranging one side of the room. There were pink pillows everywhere. A sparkly pink lamp sat on the desk next to a laptop and printer.

The laptop was also pink.

I blinked and shifted self-consciously on my feet.

"Hi."

The blonde looked up with a friendly smile that quickly faded. She stared at me like I was a bug on the wall. Maybe I was.

"Hi. Krista, right?"

The girl was looking me over and obviously finding me lacking. I noticed she was staring at my shoes and lack of luggage.

Great. Here we go again.

I sighed, already resigned to being the odd girl out.

Nothing had changed after all.

I knew I looked like a wet rat at a pedigree dog show. That was the one of the reasons I kept to myself for the most part back home. That and the strange things that seemed to happen around me.

I'd most likely keep to myself here, new start or not.

It was just easier that way.

Plus, I didn't want anyone to figure out just how different I *really* was.

"Yes, I'm Krista. Are you Charisse?"

The girl nodded slowly. "It's pronounced Charrr-eeese."

"Okay."

I set down my bags and started unpacking. Charisse went back to doing the same. And that was that.

CHAPTER 5

DEAN

"We're so proud of you, Son."

"Thanks Mom, Dad."

I hugged my mother then shook my father's hand with the firm grip I knew was expected. My mother kissed my cheeks, trying to hide the tears that were in her eyes. I watched as they got into the rented van and drove off. I was ashamed to admit how relieved I was when the taillights disappeared from view.

Not that I wouldn't miss them, at least in theory. My mother anyway. My father and I barely spoke as it was. He wanted me to excel in everything I did, and I gave him no complaints in sports or school. So he left me alone.

We both preferred it that way.

For the first time in my life, I would be free from his expectations. He wanted me to be something that I wasn't all that sure I wanted to be.

The Golden Boy. The Prodigal Son. The American Dream.

The truth was, I wanted to stand on my own two feet for once in my life. Who I was exactly... well, I wasn't in a rush to figure that out. Besides, I had a feeling that was still to be determined.

I could be a good person, and make something of myself. Or I could just as easily go down the road to rich douchenozzle land.

"Heads up, big D!"

My hands came up and closed around the bottle of cold beer one of my new roommates had just chucked out the window. Already there was music blaring. They must have been waiting for my parents to leave. I smiled and climbed the stairs to the suite.

I took one look around and shook my head.

This was going to be interesting.

A lot had happened in the ten minutes I'd been outside. Six or seven guys were sprawled on the sofas drinking out of plastic red cups and beer bottles. They were throwing footballs around the room while one guy flipped through what looked like a vast array of porn channels.

Apparently, the suite came with an extensive cable package.

I knocked the top off my beer and took a swig.

"Hey, man! Welcome to the pussy palace. You are going to get so much tail here, you have no idea."

A finger poked me in the chest and I grunted.

"You, my friend are going to be swimming in it."

I smiled and lifted my drink. There was a huge bowl full of condoms on the dining room table. I didn't say a word, though I thought it was a little bit crass to have them out in the open like that.

These guys acted like they'd never been with a girl before.

That had never really been a problem for me. Girls already threw themselves at me on a daily basis back in high school. And that was before I was on a nationally ranked college team.

I wasn't too worried about getting a girl if I wanted one. The one girl I wanted was literally impossible to get. But that was because she wasn't even real.

To be honest, all this posturing looked pretty desperate.

Not that I was going to say that. I wasn't an idiot after all. Nobody needed to know that I believed in being a gentleman instead of racking up as many hook-ups as possible.

I needed to be a part of the team and eventually if all went well, the leader. I wasn't going to start out by being a wet blanket or telling them they sounded like pigs.

I *was* hoping this wasn't a nightly occurrence though. We had our first practice in the morning. And I was here to get a degree too, not just a beer gut.

I made small talk while I finished my drink and went into my room to unpack. I had to de-Mommify my room.

I was not going to be the rich kid with matching decorative pillows on my first damn day.

CHAPTER 6

KRISTA

I heaved the huge stainless steel tub of mashed potatoes off the rolling metal caddy. It was at least thirty pounds of hot, steaming buttery goodness. I could smell it as I lowered it into the service counter.

Man, these athletes eat well...

There was nothing like this at the dining hall where I got my three meals a day. I knew I was lucky to get this assignment. The food in the dorm sucked.

And I could have been assigned there, staring my dorm mates in the face while I dished out sub-human food. I could see the cartoon version of it, with the students as wild animals, ready to eat anything that moved.

No, this was much, *much* better.

I was well aware that I'd landed one of the better work study slots, not that it was glamorous by any stretch of the imagination. Someone in the work study department must have taken a liking to me. I adjusted the cap covering my hair and retied my apron.

No, definitely not glamorous.

Or easy.

My muscles were already aching and I'd only been there for two hours of the six-hour shift. But there was a bright side to working in the athletic complex on the other side of campus. A really, really big bright side.

When you served the athletes, you got to eat what they ate. And they ate *extremely* well. Filet mignon, roast chicken, salmon and rice and steamed veggies for almost every meal. Eggs benedict with roasted ham most mornings. It was a far cry from what they served in the dorms. Which was mostly warmed over lasagna and wilted salads.

Yuck.

Oh yeah, working in the athletic center was a prized job for all the work study students.

Somehow, I'd lucked into the work slot twice a week, with a third 'floater' shift that took me where they needed me on campus. Catering special events on the weekends mostly. I'd already done a few meet and greets for various departments, serving booze to professors and department heads.

So far, those weren't bad either.

This was my first shift at the athletic center. The staff had been prepping and cooking since before I got there. Now the doors were open and it was time to serve. Another two hours and we'd close down. Then we would get a chance to eat the leftovers before clean up. Real food. As good as Nan made, or even better, just because of sheer amount of high quality meat.

My stomach growled audibly from the delicious smells filling the room.

The players were starting to filter in now, standing in line. My manager handed me a scooper and I took my position in front of the mashed potatoes. They were real ones too, made with real butter and boiled potatoes. I hadn't had any that weren't from a mix since I was a little girl. Nan didn't make them, but my mother had. I was looking forward to tasting the fluffy white concoction.

The only downside to the gig were the people I was there to serve. There was so much testosterone in the room, I could almost smell it. Big hulking guys that I was trying not to look at when they came to my station.

Thankfully for the most part, they just held out their trays and grunted.

More than once I felt eyes on me. The players walked down the line, mostly saying nothing. I kept my head down, even when one of them tried to make conversation.

He wasn't the last one either.

I was adept at side-stepping male attention for the most part. Boys seemed to act the fool around me more often than not. I'd learned to tune them out. Usually they gave up and moved on pretty quick without encouragement.

I wasn't fooled by flattery. Pretty didn't get you too far in this world. Smart was much better. Besides, I didn't have the time or inclination to date.

For the most part, I was able to ignore the players, not even bothering to spare them a glance. They were just another part of the scenery, even if they did make me a bit nervous.

It was times like these I really wished I wasn't an intuitive, as Nan called it. I could feel their halfhearted interest, and it was purely animalistic at best.

It certainly wasn't that I was putting out flirtatious vibes with my outfit. There was no way I looked hot in the uniform and plastic gloves. But apparently, I was cute enough for them to make a token effort.

That or they were starved for female companionship, which I highly doubted.

I never really thought too much about my looks. Nan had taught me not to put stock in being pretty. But I knew where I stood on the teenage food chain. It was hard not to, even if I hadn't always picked up on other people's moods and thoughts.

Trust me, that was not always a good thing.

I was sort of in the middle from what I picked up. I figured that was due to good genes. My mother had been beautiful, in a fragile, ethereal way. I knew I looked a lot like her. But I wasn't too high on the ladder because of my worn-out clothes and lack of makeup.

I hadn't even gone to my prom.

No, I was much more comfortable like this.

As usual I wore an oversized t-shirt and tight jeans. A stained apron was tied loosely over my clothes. My hair was tucked into an old baseball cap they'd given me and I decided I would get my own hat from the student center bookshop for next time. It was worth the splurge.

But for today it was the old hat, or the dreaded hair net. The hat was a minor upgrade. But there was no way I looked appealing.

And yet I got a steady stream of 'hey baby's' and even one 'aren't you a cutie.'

I was not impressed. I knew they were probably just bored. They were after one thing and one thing only. And they weren't getting it from me.

Nan always said that testosterone could do crazy things to a man, no matter how old he was.

I didn't really care to find out.

I sighed and doled out another scoop of mashed potatoes. It was monotonous to say the least. I risked a glance at the clock to see how much time had passed until I could eat.

Not enough.

I noticed the quiet and looked up. The line had stopped. But that wasn't what made my breath catch in my throat.

There was a boy standing in front of me. He was extremely handsome, with wavy brown hair and blue green eyes. He wasn't a hulk like the rest of the jocks. He was tall and well built. Strong looking, but not bulky.

He was staring at me with a look of shock on his chiseled face. His *familiar* face. His familiar stormy blue eyes.

Not just any eyes.

His eyes.

It was him. The boy from my dreams. The boy I'd been dreaming about for literally years was standing in front of me, looking as shocked as I felt.

"You're real."

His voice was husky and full of wonder. His lips curled into a smile and I gasped, the full ramifications of what this meant slamming home.

This wasn't real. He was not real. It could not be happening.

THIS COULD NOT BE HAPPENING.

But it was happening. Right now. And I had no idea what to do about it.

My famous coping mechanisms flew out the window. I froze, unable to move or even speak. I could barely *think.*

My chest felt dry and tight, I realized I hadn't taken a breath in what felt like minutes. My fingers gripped the edge of the counter as I struggled to get a deep breath.

I blinked at him as he shook his head and smiled. His lips opened and I realized he was trying to talk to me.

But I didn't want to hear it.

I dropped my serving spoon into the mashed potatoes and ran into the kitchen. I didn't stop. I ran straight out the service entrance and into the cool evening air.

CHAPTER 7

DEAN

S*he was real.*

I stood there, holding onto my tray for dear life as time seemed to stop. It was like I was on Mars all of the sudden. Everything around me felt that strange. That foreign.

In the blink of an eye, everything I'd ever known, everything I had assumed was reality had been proved wrong.

She was *real*.

My heart was pounding as I stood there in a stupor. Someone said something and I snapped out of it, pushing my tray down the line. I felt like I was in a dream.

A dream, but not *the* dream.

And yet... she was here.

My whole world had just been turned upside down. And I'd never been happier in my entire life. A feeling of pure euphoria washed through me, making me light up like a Christmas tree.

I was ecstatic at having my illusions shattered. Most people might not be. They held onto 'facts' with everything they had. But I was ready to shout it out, make sure everyone knew.

Dear god, the beautiful girl from my dreams was *real*.

My world had tilted as I stared into the huge gray eyes I'd seen so often in my sleep. I hadn't just been dreaming her up after all. I'd been seeing a real girl somehow, not a beautiful figment of my imagination.

She was real and she was here, working in the cafeteria. What were the chances of that? There probably wasn't even a number for calculating those odds.

But that wasn't even the crazy part.

The crazy part was the look in her eyes. She had looked as shocked as I was. I knew without a doubt that she'd recognized me too.

She knew me just as surely as I knew her.

I just didn't know her name.

I had tried to open my mouth to get the words out — what words, I wasn't sure of just yet — but the overwhelming feeling in my gut had been of completion. Shock and awe yes, but also a wonderful, miraculous feeling of having found something I'd lost.

I felt whole for the first time in my life.

Then reality started to set in. My mystery girl looked less than thrilled to see me. Her pretty face was in shock, leaving two bright pink spots on her cheeks. For all my surprise, she looked even more rattled than I felt.

I had a sudden need to reassure her — I needed to—

But she ran.

I stared as the girl turned and scurried into the back of the kitchens. But I knew I had seen the look of recognition in her face.

The shock and the... something else. Joy almost. But she'd looked horrified as well.

Okay, so that wasn't the joyous reunion I might have hoped for. But for the first time in forever, I didn't feel alone.

Even though she'd just run out of there like her shoes were on fire.

"She's hot, right? I'd like to unload on her ass."

I cringed. My suitemate Chuck was not subtle about women. All he talked about were stats and how to get girls. As many as possible. And now he was talking about *her* in the same way.

I didn't like it. I didn't like it at all.

I set my tray down on a table and walked purposefully toward the kitchen. A heavyset middle-aged woman with red hair stood in my way. She might be an adult, but I was taller.

I looked down at her, impatient to get past her. I was ready to fight dragons to get to that girl, let alone stop and talk. But my good manners won out.

"Excuse me, please."

"You can't be back here, son. Can I get you something?"

"The girl who was here — did she leave? I need to talk to her."

"Krista? I think she just went out back for air."

"Okay, thanks."

I walked swiftly out of the front of the building and jogged to the back where the employee entrance was. I walked around the loading dock and dumpsters. But there was no one there.

She was gone.

It didn't matter though. I knew her name now. I knew where she worked, and I knew she was a student here. I would find her, soon.

My whole body was thrumming with the possibility of seeing her again soon. Talking to her. Kissing her. And I wouldn't have to fall asleep to do it.

She was here.

She was real.

CHAPTER 8

KRISTA

"Cute outfit."

I stopped in the doorway, staring at my roommate. Charisse was looking at me like I was the Loch Ness monster. I had just walked in the door and already I wanted to hide.

Everyone was staring at me today. The players, my roommate, *him*. I didn't like it.

I stared down at myself, wondering what was wrong with me now.

Oh, right. Brilliant, Krista.

Whoops. I'd forgotten to take the apron off. It was a nicer one, a dark green made for serving in the front of the kitchen. But it was still less than glamorous.

Not to mention splattered with small bits of mashed potatoes and regret.

Fantastic. I was wearing part of the dinner I hadn't gotten a chance to even taste. Because I hadn't finished my shift. Because I was ridiculous. And now I would go to bed hungry because of it.

Brilliant Krista.

I pulled off the apron, tempted to throw it away. I wanted to bury it. Just hide the evidence of my foolishness. I only hoped I wouldn't get fired for running out of there like that. Not to mention looking like a freak as I ran through campus.

Yeah, this whole 'new life' thing was off to a fantastic start.

I couldn't lose my job. Not now. Not ever. For four years, my work study was a privilege as well as a burden. It was part of my arrangement with the scholarship office. I would have to tell them I'd gotten sick or something. Otherwise I was screwed.

No work study, no partial scholarship, no college. The rules were very clear on that.

Way to go, Krista.

I sighed and pulled the apron off, hanging it on the hook on the back of the door.

"You smell like French fries."

"Mashed potatoes, actually. One of the many hazards of work study. I'll get cleaned up."

Charisse wrinkled her nose and tossed me something. I stared at the expensive looking bottle in my hand. Rose scented shower gel.

Well, that was subtle.

"Here. My mother gets me buckets of this stuff. You look like a rose girl."

She held up another bottle.

"I'm more of a lemon verbena girl myself. You can have all the rose stuff."

"Um… Thanks."

I took a sniff and shrugged. It did smell better than my plain soap and drug store moisturizer. And the scent was familiar, in a bittersweet way.

My mother had always smelled like roses.

Charisse chucked matching shampoo, conditioner and a dry body oil onto my bed. She murmured something about wanting to stuff her face now and I almost laughed. She wasn't mean exactly, but she wasn't sweet either.

I grabbed my shower caddy, adding all the rose scented stuff and shuffled to the dorm bathroom.

In my case 'dorm shower caddy' was an old rubber bucket that had been under my Grandmother's sink forever. Nan had raised me on a strict, extremely limited income. We used what we had.

I kind of liked it that way too. Just looking at the waste and excess around the dorm was a little dizzying, to tell the truth. But I couldn't judge people for having money, just like I hoped they didn't judge me for… not.

I knew they did judge me though. I might not react to the stares and whispers, but I always noticed them. I knew I didn't quite belong.

Never had. Never would.

Even here at this top school, where we were all supposedly intelligent over-achievers, I was still just the girl from the wrong side of the tracks. The girl who had to work just to stay in classes. The girl who smelled like French fries.

I'd even heard a couple of them call me hillbilly Barbie. Gee, thanks. I put those people on my ignore list. Permanently.

I padded down the hall in my shower shoes — also-known-as 99 cent flip flops. I looked around the communal bathroom, relieved that it was not crowded for once. I was shy about showering around other girls, even if we were all in the same boat.

I pulled off my clothes and stepped into the shower stall. The water was steaming hot and the pressure was good. One of the few perks of communal showering I supposed: the boiler was industrial sized.

I poured some of the expensive gel into my hand and inhaled deeply. It did smell pretty good actually, especially compared to the plain bar soap I'd used to wash my face and body every day since I was five.

I went through the motions of washing myself off on autopilot. But the truth was the silence was deafening. Now I had nothing to distract me from the truth. The one thought was running through my head on repeat.

The one thought I'd been fighting ever since I'd run out of the dining hall almost an hour ago.

He was real.

CHAPTER 9

DEAN

My eyes slipped to the side, resting on the dark, wavy hair again. The hair that was shorter than I remembered. Everything else was the same.

I sat in Freshman Lit, forcing myself to stare blankly towards the front of the lecture hall. It was the third day of classes. I'd spent every day since Freshman orientation looking for her. She hadn't appeared in the kitchen again and I hadn't seen her in the quad.

I was beginning to think I'd imagined the whole thing.

Until now.

Two rows ahead of me and a few seats to the right. A girl sat there that drew my eye repeatedly during the class. He could see her profile and the shoulder length dark hair that curled around her ear perfectly, revealing a graceful jaw and neck.

Her hand fluttered to her throat as if she felt eyes on her. My breath caught as she glanced over her shoulder as if she knew someone was watching her. I glanced away, unconcerned.

I wasn't the only one checking her out. Krista drew male eyes like moths to a flame. It wasn't just her beauty either. She looked fragile too, in a way that brought out his protective instincts.

The girl from my dreams was pretty much a man-magnet.

And it *was* her.

I was not crazy after all.

I leaned back and smiled grimly, letting my eyes rest on her again. I had to talk to her- to make her stay this time. Not run away. She had to know we were meant to be together.

Well, maybe I was a *little* bit crazy.

I had started to stand in the middle of class the moment I saw her face. I sat down abruptly, realizing looking like a crazy person was not going to help my cause . I had to get to her, to speak to her, not make her run away again.

It was her, but she was different.

Her hair was longer in the dreams, and her clothes were different. She was dressed kind of shabbily compared to the plain white nightgown I was used to seeing her in.

It was the sort of nightie that you saw in old movies. White cotton and lace. Virginal.

For some reason I had always found it incredibly arousing. In fact, just holding her hand in the dreams was more satisfying than any of the fumbling sexual encounters I'd had in high school.

I felt it now, a fission of desire that went straight to my gut. I shifted uncomfortably in my seat, eager to get on with it.

I'm going to make her talk to me, one way or the other.

The bell rang and she was up like a shot. I cursed when I saw her making a beeline for the door. I couldn't let her get away again.

I stood up and chased after her, pushing people out of the way.

I shoved way through the crowd, finally catching up to her. I lifted my arm and touched her shoulder just as she stepped out of the building.

She turned and her stunning gray eyes widened. She stepped away from me, almost stumbling down the stairs. I reached out for her and steadied her.

Nice Dean, knock your dream girl down the freaking stairs why don't you? Classy.

The next thing I knew she had darted out into the crowd of milling students on the quad. She was pretty fast for such a little thing. I followed her, unwilling to give up so easily.

"Wait- Krista- I just need to talk to you-"

Jesus Christ, the girl was motoring!

She ignored me, weaving through the crowd of students until she stopped short, blocked by a game of catch football. I grabbed her shoulder and turned her to face me. Not the smoothest move in the book, but I was desperate.

"I know you."

Her big eyes blinked up at me from her heart shaped face. I knew instantly that she was about to lie to me. Even before she opened that beautiful mouth of hers.

"I don't know what you're talking about. I've never seen you before in my life."

"Yes, you have."

I stared at her, my hands firm on her shoulders.

"It's okay. I'm freaked too. This whole thing- it's crazy."

She got perfectly still, staring at the ground as if willing me to go away. Then she shook her head, as if she was trying to clear it.

"Yeah, okay. I guess you're right."

My heart was clanging in my chest as she took a deep breath and looked up at me. Her beautiful gray eyes were lost and I had to fight the desire to pull her into my arms.

"It *is* crazy. I think I'm going crazy."

I smiled at her.

"Maybe we both are."

CHAPTER 10

KRISTA

He was beautiful. Not just his looks. Everything about him was just... perfect.

My heart was beating so fast, it felt like it was a horse that might gallop away from me. He wasn't just here. He was demanding that I talk to him, that I admit what was happening.

God help me, I wanted to talk to him too.

I wanted everything in the dreams to be real. The long walks. The handholding. The kiss.

Especially the kiss.

But something inside me warned that there would be consequences if I gave into that desire. That this chance — this boy — he was not a free gift. I didn't know if it was just nerves, or a lifetime of being the odd girl out, but my internal warning bell was clanging and it was *loud.*

I let myself look at him, momentarily silencing the voice inside me that told me to run. I just... *looked.* My eyes drank him in like the tall, cool drink of water that he was.

Oh my goodness, the boy was fine.

His eyes were exactly the same as I remembered, his shoulders just as broad. His hair was shorter, cut for the upcoming football season most likely. I missed the tousled curls he'd had the last time I saw him. It softened him somehow.

Now he looked... hard.

Determined.

He was staring at me, begging me with those deep blue eyes to say the words that would make this all real.

Too real.

Once I said it out loud though, I wouldn't be able to take them back. It was a line in the sand. I realized with a sense of inevitability that nothing would stop me from crossing it.

Maybe this was fate. Maybe it was magic. Real magic, not the kind you read about in fairy tales. Either way, I couldn't fight it any longer.

I sighed, unable to resist the entreating look in his beautiful eyes.

"Your hair is shorter."

He smiled at me with such relief that it almost made it worth it. Even when we both ended up in the loony bin.

Almost.

"Yours too."

I ran my hand through my new haircut distractedly.

"Yeah, well my Nan cut it. She wanted to make the cut last until I went home again for Thanksgiving break."

He was just standing there, staring at me. Not like I was a freak though. He looked like a kid on Christmas morning. Then he held out his hand expectantly. I looked at it as if it were a snake that might bite me.

"I'm Dean."

Dean. The name suited him. It was strong.

I sighed, ignoring his hand. I had to make it clear to him that this was a one-time conversation. I was here to study. not to chat with mysterious dream boys.

"Look, this isn't a good idea. We should just act like none of this ever happened. Otherwise we are basically admitting that we are insane."

"Like I said, maybe we are. I'm okay with that."

He was still grinning when he said it. I sighed again, feeling like I was speaking to a slow-witted child.

Except he wasn't, was he? He was a big, beautiful looking young man. An Adonis really. How could he be here talking to me? I was so sure I'd conjured him up out of loneliness all those years ago.

He was supposed to just be my imaginary boyfriend dammit.

"Come on, let's talk about it. What's the big deal?"

"The big deal—"

I lowered my voice, whispering at him as I started walking around the outskirts of the game again.

"The big deal is that stuff like this isn't supposed to happen."

"Yeah, it's weird. But it's *good* weird, you know?"

I stopped and stared at him. He was so solid. So *actually there in the flesh* that I had to resist the urge to reach out and poke him.

"I guess."

"So, are you going to admit this is happening or what?"

I sighed again and stared at the hand he was once again holding out. He just stood there, patiently waiting for me to accept it. I reached out and slid my small hand into his.

"Krista. I'm Krista."

He smiled at me and clasped my hand firmly. A jolt shot through me, rattling my bones. He jerked as if he felt it too.

It was like an electrical current that seared the flesh of my palm, and shot straight to the soles of my feet. I let go abruptly, reaching up to touch the top of my head.

My hair was sticking straight up.

Dean's was too.

He smiled sheepishly as if that were a totally normal reaction to a handshake.

"So… Can I buy you a cup of coffee, Krista?"

CHAPTER 11

DEAN

This was happening. Finally, she was sitting still and letting me get a good look at her.

It was hard to hide my grin. I stared stupidly at the ridiculously adorable girl sitting across the cafe table from me. The ridiculously adorable girl who shouldn't even exist.

But she *did* exist. And God damn if I wasn't thrilled about it.

I felt like I'd just won the jackpot.

Krista, on the other hand, looked nervous. Conflicted. Miserable, even. As if she'd rather be anywhere but here.

I didn't care about her misgivings at the moment, though. I was too ecstatic. I would just have to find a way to convince her that it was a good idea to get to know me. A *very* good idea.

I could do it too. I would turn on the charm, be the perfect suitor. I'd done it a thousand times with teachers and parents. I could certainly convince this shy little girl that I was boyfriend material. Just as long as she didn't run off again.

From zero to boyfriend in under sixty seconds.

Damn if I didn't want to be just that. Didn't matter how long it took. I'd never chased a girl in my life but this was different. *Krista was different.* I knew I'd do just about anything to make this girl mine.

Something occurred to me and I blurted out the words "You don't have a boyfriend, do you?" without even thinking. I was flooded with relief when she shook her head.

"Where are you from? I never get to see your... house."

I smirked at the blush that lit up her cheeks at the reminder. I wanted her to remember how intimate her nocturnal visits were. Innocent, but definitely personal.

She visited me in my bedroom often, but it was never the other way around. I smiled. I'd give anything to see the inside of her bedroom right about now.

"Louisiana."

"I'm from New Hampshire."

"Oh, I thought so."

"How did you know?"

She shrugged, her dainty shoulders rising apologetically.

"I can sort of tell which way I'm going. Even if it's not deliberate."

"Oh, so you didn't come looking for me on purpose?"

She blushed deeper and shook her head.

"No— I just sort of— find myself there."

I grinned wider as she turned even redder if that was possible. And then she stood up, clearly deciding the date was over. I was on my feet in a half a second, ready to follow her wherever she went.

Even if it was just to the ladies' room.

"Look, I should get back. Lots of homework and stuff."

That was bullshit. She was just trying to get out of the date. I raised an eyebrow and called her on it.

"It's the first week of school. There no way you have a lot of homework."

She looked away. I still had a stupid smile on my face. Even though she was trying to get away from me. I knew I probably looked like a fool but I didn't care.

"Yeah, but I have to work tomorrow so I need to do my homework tonight."

"Okay. Let me walk you."

She gave me a wary glance that said, 'I am onto you.'

This time I hid my smile. She was right. I did want to know which dorm she lived in. Anyway, it worked.

I followed her doggedly, keeping up a steady stream of chatter. She answered me cautiously, as if she was afraid to reveal too much of herself. Instead of annoying me for some reason I found it adorable, and slightly mysterious. Just like she was.

It was only a short walk to one of the large freshman dorms that lined the edges of campus. I stared up at Tanner Hall and smiled. Now I knew where to find her.

Bingo.

"Can I see you again soon?"

"Uh, yeah okay."

Relief flooded my system. That had been easy.

"How about tomorrow?"

She shrugged.

"I work at the dining hall, remember? I'll be there tomorrow. You can lay eyes on me."

I grinned at her. She was being deliberately obtuse. She was so damned beautiful!

"No, I mean like this. On a date."

Her pretty lips popped open. I'd shocked her. Again.

"This was a date?"

I smiled wider and leaned toward her. I wanted to kiss those pretty lips. Hell, I wanted to do more than that.

Much much more.

Her eyes got as big as saucers as I got closer. She turned her head at the last possible moment, leaving me to kiss her cheek.

That was okay though. I was in the perfect spot to whisper in her ear, "Yes, Krista. It was."

She stared up at me, looking dazed.

"It was what?"

"A date."

CHAPTER 12

KRISTA

A *date. He wanted to go on a date with me.*

I stood up and then sat down again, jumping back up immediately. I realized what I was doing and started pacing back and forth on my side of the room instead. I was always careful to try not and intrude on my roommate's side, but right now I wanted to run laps around the room.

Maybe bounce off the ceiling too.

Haha, Krista. That would not go over too well.

"You okay?"

"Uh huh. I'm great. Never better."

Charisse gave me an odd look from her bed where she was lounging on a mound of pillows. She looked like a queen over there. A queen with an affection for pink.

Didn't matter if she thought I was crazy. I could not seem to sit still. I wasn't sure what to do with myself.

He'd tried to kiss me. Just like in the dream. But this was better.

That gorgeous, impossibly real boy had tried to kiss me *for real.*

Only I'd turned my head at the last second. *Because I was an idiot.* He'd taken it in stride but the moment was ruined. But at least I'd avoided disaster, right? I wanted this to fade away, not encourage him.

Um… Why had I done that again?

Oh right, because this was all madness and we were clearly headed for the insane asylum.

Repeat it to yourself, Krista: kissing him would only make things worse. Well, not during the kiss. That would be nice. But after.

Post-kiss bedlam.

I stared at my desk until I realized the pages of my sketchbook were flipping. Without me touching them. I leaned forward and pressed my hands down on it but it had already stilled.

In fact, it had stopped on a sketch I had done right before coming here. A sketch of Dean. A sketch I drew before I even met him in real life.

What was happening to me?

I'd always known I was a bit odd. Different somehow. Nan had called me 'special' which had sounded good until I'd realized that often meant something entirely different.

So, special didn't quite fit either. My feet were firmly on the ground. When I was awake, anyway. I was a sensible, hardworking young woman.

Everybody knew that. I got straight A's. I worked hard. I did my chores. I never complained.

So why did I feel like crying my eyes out because a cute guy had tried to kiss me?

Because I was crazy. I shook my head. One thing I definitely did not have, was loose screws.

But I did have this odd ability to travel in my dreams. It was a real thing, though not all that common. I'd looked it up.

It's called astral projection apparently. But my nightly journeys seemed to go way beyond what the spiritual blogs described. It was supposed to be rare, even for people who did special meditations to achieve it.

So basically, I was a freak.

I never told a soul about the astral-whatever. Or the way small animals followed me around. Charisse had commented already on the birds that woke us up every morning. She'd wanted to shoo them away but I stopped her.

They were sweet. And they were just saying hello.

So why did I want to chase Dean away again? If I could deal with the birds and butterflies, why not a six-foot hunk?

Because he was different. He was connected to the dreams somehow, and that scared me.

I had never encountered the same person more than once. Oh, I did come across people now and then. They usually did not see me, or acknowledge me in anyway. I had a feeling they were usually half asleep. Or had just a trace of the abilities I had.

So, not one soul knew what I could do. Not my mother. And not even Nan.

Except for him.

I sat down heavily on the bed, remembering the first time I'd found myself in his room. I'd been drawn there without knowing why, just staring down at this beautiful boy. He'd opened his eyes. He'd *seen* me.

And smiled.

It had been like a shock to the system. After that, I hadn't been alone anymore. Somehow, just like that, we were together.

And now he was real, and he wanted to kiss me. Did he really want to date me? Sleep with me? I didn't know. I had never felt more vulnerable and exposed in my life.

For the first time, someone knew about me. My darkest secret. Someone *normal*. Oh yeah, he was mainstream. Dean was as true blue American as they came.

He should have been freaked out by the weird, dream-invading girl from the wrong side of the tracks.

But he wasn't.

In fact, he didn't seem to mind at all. He even seemed to like me for some reason, freakish nighttime abilities and all.

Of course, he didn't know the half of it. How far I travelled. How sometimes I seemed to know things before they happened, even when I was awake. How my hands got hot when I touched someone who was ailing.

Nan called it 'healing hands' and credited her vitality at seventy-five to my touch. I'd even laid hands on a dying bird in the backyard once. It had chirped at me and flown away.

Not far though. The silly bird came back to visit all the time for the next few years, reminding me of all the things that were wrong with me.

Unnatural things. And those things had been getting worse.

Dean didn't know any of that.

And he wasn't going to find out. *Ever.* Even if I did see him again, which I was very tempted to do. It was a terrible idea.

A terrible, wonderful, seductively dangerous idea.

I hadn't answered him about the date. Tomorrow I would see if there was another shift I could take. I hated to give up the good grub but it was for the best. Somewhere else on campus other than the sports complex. Anywhere else.

Then there would just be class to contend with. I could switch but— I sighed.

Who was I kidding?

I couldn't run from this. I couldn't run from *him.* And I wasn't even sure I wanted to. My feet felt as heavy as lead when he was around, especially when I was running away. I

51

wanted to be around him, more than anything I'd ever felt before.

It was hopeless.

He already knew where I lived. He knew my name. And I could tell that he wasn't going to give up, no matter how many times I deflected his advances.

The scariest part was, I wasn't sure I wanted him to give up. Even if it was dangerous, and oh-so-stupid.

Once I'd admitted that to myself, I finally calmed down. I was thoughtful as I got ready for bed. I climbed in, bringing my sketchpad with me. It might seem odd to curl up with a pencil and a smudged up old pad of paper, but for once I didn't care what Charisse or anyone else thought.

I relied on my sketches as a link to the dream world. I would often draw what I saw when I woke up early in the morning or even in the middle of the night. It was like a record of my second life, one I hoped would someday make sense of my gift.

I had shoeboxes full of drawings at home. I'd just started this fresh sketch pad over the summer. It was already more than halfway full. There were half a dozen pictures of Dean inside it. He was that prominent in my dreams.

I opened the book again and stared at the one I'd drawn a few weeks ago. I stared at the drawing, not remembering the dream at all. It took me a moment to figure out what was bothering me about the finely drawn sketch.

When I realized what it was I gasped, dropping my pad as if it was on fire. The pages fluttered and I found myself staring, almost unable to look away.

All the pages were covered in black and white, plain graphite on paper. But not this sketch.

In this one drawing, Dean's eyes were red.

CHAPTER 13

DEAN

The sky was dark and churning with clouds. I sat up in my suite, immediately aware that I was dreaming. I stared at my hand, turning it this way and that.

I was glowing faintly. I turned back and saw myself turn over in bed.

Yeah, dreaming. Like I did when Krista came. But... not. Because she was nowhere to be found.

I turned in a circle, wondering what the hell I was supposed to do now. I glanced at the window and froze.

Someone was outside in the parking lot.

I ran to the window, nearly slamming into it. Right. Dream movements were a bit more erratic.

Slow your roll, Dean.

Then I saw her. A woman was down there, facing away. Staring up at the moon.

Krista.

I ran down the stairs, moving faster than I ever could in real life. I bounced against the wall as I took a corner too hard. I'd never tried to go anywhere in the dream before. It was going to take some getting used to.

I reached for the door, cursing as my hand was unable to grasp it. So, walls were solid, but I couldn't grab the damn door?

Fantastic.

I blinked and suddenly I was outside, inches away from her. I stared at her slender back, and the soft waves that

53

seemed even longer than usual. My fingers slid through them, reaching for her shoulder.

She turned.

It was not Krista.

She looked a hell of a lot like her though.

I frowned, staring at her in confusion. The woman was older, but still beautiful. Her features were softer than Krista's but so similar I could not look away.

She spoke to me without opening her mouth. Her voice was sweet and so sad it broke my heart. But what she said made me rear back in fear and anger. I ran into the building without even pausing to try the door.

A moment later I sat up in my bed. I remembered everything. The woman. My panic at her words.

Everything but what she told me.

CHAPTER 14

KRISTA

Here we go again.

I grabbed the dirty apron and folded it into a neat roll, almost eager to get to work. I was full of a strange energy today. My dreams had been extra active and had woken me at dawn.

Last night, I'd gone traveling farther than ever before.

I hadn't been able to fall back asleep, all the images inside me screaming to be let out, recorded, made sense of.

Plus, I knew I would see him again today.

I'd given up on sleep early, sitting in bed and working on my sketch pad. Once I'd realized Dean wasn't making an appearance in my dream, I'd gone exploring on my own.

I'd checked up on Nan, who always seemed to smile when I was in the room with her. I didn't know if she sensed me or not. She never said a word about it. She'd give a funny smile, as if she knew a secret, but that was all. Even if she was asleep, Nan would get restless when I came to visit.

I had left quickly, afraid to disturb the older woman. Nan needed her sleep, which was harder to come by at her age. Instead I wound up at the beach again, somewhere on the East Coast.

Not just any beach. It was his beach. Dean's.

But he wasn't here. As far I knew, he didn't travel in his dreams. Not without me.

A seal was lounging on the sand, and I stopped to pet it. It rolled its neck, pressing its silky head into my palm. Seals

55

were one of my favorite animals, friendly and sociable. They were kind of like the puppies of the sea.

As usual, the animals I encountered seemed to see me, even though people did not. Every once in a while, I might encounter someone who could see me but it was rare. Usually a young child, and even then, it was only for an instant. Never anything like Dean.

I sighed, hurrying even though I was technically early for my shift. Something strange was going on between us whether I liked it or not. I wasn't sure what it was yet, but I had little doubt that I'd find out.

Whether I wanted to or not. Destiny was funny that way. Or at least, that was one of the things Nan always said.

For the moment at least, I was stuck with Dean.

I hid a smile. There were worse things than being stuck with someone who looked like Dean. And he wasn't just handsome. He was intrinsically a good person. Inside and out.

True, we hadn't talked all that much but I could tell when I looked into his eyes.

Either way, it was clear that I wasn't going to be able to just blow him off at this point. He knew where to find me, even in my sleep apparently.

That had been a first.

Last night, right before waking, he'd shown up. It had been three days since I laid eyes on him, but I still hadn't been scared.

Somehow, it had made me feel even more secure. He knew where to find me. He would look after me. He really did want to be with me.

And now I was on my way back to the field house, where he'd be in the flesh. He'd give me that crooked grin and try to get me to see him after my shift.

I wasn't using precognition to guess that. It was just his style to be direct and persistent. Just like it was my style to hide and protect.

Hunter and prey.

I pushed open the door to the service entrance and slipped the dirty apron into a laundry bin unnoticed. My manager was a warm older woman named Pam. After a stilted explanation, Pam stared at me for a brief moment before breaking out in a big smile.

"Think nothing of it, sweetheart."

"Thanks, Pam. And sorry."

I'd been tempted to ask her if I could stay in the back, working the blazing hot dishwasher instead of the service line. But I held my tongue for some reason. Besides, this time I wouldn't be caught off guard.

This time, I wanted to see Dean.

There. I'd finally said it.

I wanted to see him.

CHAPTER 15

DEAN

"Goodnight, man."

I nodded at my teammates as I walked out of the dining hall. I'd sat there long enough, watching Krista serve and slowly eating my food. I stayed to the end of the shift making sure no one hassled her, halfheartedly thumbing through one of my assignments.

I headed to the back when they started closing up, standing under a tree near the exit. I sniffed the air, and moved further away. The trash was out here and it was overpowering, even from twenty feet away,

It seemed like I could smell everything lately and it wasn't always pleasant. It was getting worse too. I'd been noticing it all day.

Right now, the dumpster felt like it was right next to me. Actually, it felt like it was inside my damn nose. I rubbed it and winced.

I felt a breeze coming from the North and lifted my chin to sniff at the air. I looked up, realizing the air was cleaner above. In two minutes I was in the air, staring down from my perch in the tree.

It had been years since I'd climbed a tree. Nearly a decade. And now I was fifteen feet up, without even breaking a sweat.

Somehow, climbing came as naturally as breathing to me. Just like today at practice. Everything felt simpler to me today.

Easy.

Well, everything except Krista.

She was complicated as hell.

I'd spent the entire meal watching her. Waiting in line. Accepting my food from her. Sitting and eating.

She'd smiled shyly at me. But I hadn't smiled. I'd been too intent on watching her. Keeping her safe and close.

I had a crazy urge to stick to her like glue. Almost like I wanted lock her away forever. I'd never felt this way before, or anything like it. The feeling was overpowering.

Every time I looked at her I thought one word: mine.

I didn't try to stop my possessive thoughts. I knew it was pointless to fight it.

So I sat. I ate. I watched.

And I bided my time.

Now I was outside, waiting patiently again. I didn't know exactly when her shift was over but I would be there, waiting. I wanted to be alone with her. To talk, if nothing else. To arrange for our date, when we could finally be alone together.

Uninterrupted.

This was more than just hormones.

I didn't just want anyone. It had to be her.

A startled, high-pitched sound caught my attention. I stared down at the mewling creature in my hand. A squirrel. I'd caught it without realizing what I was doing. Without even looking at it.

I tilted my head, pity and revulsion twisting in my gut.

It's squirmed frantically, desperate to get away. I felt the fragile bones in its body already breaking. I'd already killed it without meaning to. It might take hours but I knew it would not recover.

It would be kinder to kill it. Put it out of its misery. But I'd never killed anything bigger than a fly. I didn't even like to fish.

But right now… right now, it didn't really bother me.

I twisted its neck and dropped it, staring at the faint smudge of blood on my hand.

Then I heard her. My head snapped up, staring into the darkness. I let go of the branch, landing in a crouch ten feet below.

She jumped as I stood slowly, walking towards her.

"Krista."

CHAPTER 16

KRISTA

I let out a tiny scream when I saw him, then immediately relaxed. It was just Dean, not some mugger. But what was he doing out here in the middle of nowhere?

And where had he come from?

I stared upwards, realizing he'd just dropped almost twenty feet from a tree. A jump like that would have broken the legs of a lesser man. Anybody really.

Jeez, was he on 'roids or something?

I tugged on my baseball cap, suddenly feeling self-conscious. I was tired and dirty. Smelly probably. I was definitely not at my best after a six-hour shift. But the boy standing in front of me was looking at me like I was a queen.

His queen.

"Dean. Hi. What are you doing here?"

My voice squeaked like a cartoon mouse. I expected him to laugh at me for being silly but he didn't. He didn't even smile. He just stood there, staring at me.

"Waiting for you."

I laughed nervously.

"You are persistent, I'll give you that."

Again, he didn't joke along with me. I was used to him being lighthearted and teasing. But he was as still as a statue, staring at me with the same intense look on his face.

"I know what I want."

I was almost afraid to ask. But my Nan hadn't raised me to be a coward. I lifted my chin and asked.

"And what is that exactly?"

His eyes seemed to burn into me as the same thought pulsed through my veins over and over again. Something was strange. Dean was acting like he was souped-up on fifty cups of coffee or something.

He was different today.

Time seemed to stop as we stared at each other. I had that same strange thought again… it wasn't a good one either. For the second time, it occurred to me that we were predator and prey. But that didn't make sense.

Dean wouldn't hurt me, would he?

Then he smiled, and I was immediately at ease.

"Dinner with a beautiful lady."

I found myself nodding. Something about him… he was exuding power and something else… persuasion maybe. I had a strange feeling I would have said yes to anything.

Well, *almost* anything.

"You mean me?"

"Yes, I mean you."

I blushed and looked away.

"Okay."

He grinned in that lopsided way of his. The one that made my heart go pitter patter. The one that was half adorable boy and half strong young man.

This was the old Dean. Sweet and charming. A jock, for sure, but also sensitive. I felt all the tension leave my body in relief.

"Alright then. Let me walk you home."

"You don't have to."

"Yes, I do."

He was quiet on the way back to my dorm. I wanted to ask him what he meant but I had lost my nerve. I was still worried that I smelled like fried food when we got to the far side of campus.

"I'll pick you up tomorrow at seven."

He stepped closer and I froze, sure that I reeked of fries and dish soap. He didn't try and kiss me again though. His lips barely brushed my cheek.

But I felt the impact in my entire body.

He looked down at me, his eyes knowing. Like he knew that I had goosebumps all over my arms from one tiny kiss. He smiled and brushed my hair away from my face.

"Sleep well, Krista."

I watched him walk away, rooted to the spot.

I hadn't been imagining things.

Dean was different.

CHAPTER 17

DEAN

I pulled on a freshly pressed blue button down shirt and tucked it into my crisp khakis. My laundry had been delivered that morning, another one of the services provided free of charge for athletes.

I shook my head. They made things so easy for us it was ridiculous.

It was almost as good as home, though it lacked the familiar laundry scent. My mom had used some fancy organic stuff that smelled like lemons. But not having to do your own laundry was hard to complain about.

The players had a laundry service that included dry cleaning. It was stupefying, how easy the school made life for their athletes. They even had on-call tutors to help with homework. Some of them even did your homework for you, if you wanted them to.

I did not.

Unlike half of the guys who were here for sports and partying, I was in college to actually *earn* a degree. My worst nightmare was being just another stupid, rich white jerks.

Lord knows, my parents knew enough of them.

Hell, they were borderline jerks themselves. They were already rich and white. Of course, my parents were kind and loving for the most part. And smart. But still, they had moments of snobbery. They definitely weren't too far from joining the club.

There were enough RWA's back home to fill a country club with. Actually, I decided that's what they should rename the golf and beach club. I grabbed my wallet, walking through the empty townhouse.

It was blissfully quiet.

I'd somehow managed to get the nightly party to switch to another suite, just with a few pointed looks. I didn't even have to say anything. I didn't want to alienate the guys I'd be playing with for the next four years.

Thankfully, my skills on the field seemed to be enough to earn me little more than the mostly affectionate nickname of 'Rich Boy.'

I didn't mind as much as I might have a few weeks ago. The truth was, I *was* rich. It didn't really bother me one way or the other.

All I really cared about at the moment was getting close to Krista. Tonight was the first step. I'd had to ask her out three times, but three was apparently the magic number.

She'd finally said yes when I cornered her in the smelly service alley behind the field house. I was taking her to dinner tonight at the fanciest place I could find. It might be overkill, but it was important to show her that I was taking this seriously.

That I took *her* seriously.

I hadn't brought my car with me to college, thinking it was going to be a hassle. But now I was planning to pick it up the next time I went back home. If you had a girlfriend, it made sense, especially when the cold weather came.

Or maybe I'd ask my parents to bring it up for the big opening game next weekend. Then I could drive Krista wherever she wanted to go.

I grinned. That was something to look forward to, for sure.

I knocked on the door to her room and smiled when she opened it. She looked beautiful, with pale pink lip gloss enhancing her already stunning good looks. She was wearing jeans and a cardigan over an old t-shirt.

She looked horrified when she realized how dressed up I was.

"Hey."

"Hey."

"Um, so where are we going exactly?" she asked, sounding nervous.

"La Poutiserie."

"That sounds fancy…"

"It's okay, I can wait downstairs while you change."

She stared at me looking supremely uncomfortable. "I don't really… have anything fancy."

"I don't mind. Maybe just a dress?"

"I don't have one."

I felt like such an ass. I had picked up that she wasn't privileged. She had a scholarship and did work study to afford college, especially a top tier school like this one.

It had never occurred to me that she wouldn't have something to wear.

CHAPTER 18

KRISTA

W*ell, this is soul crushing.*

For the first time since arriving at school, I was thankful for the necessity of having roommates. Mine in particular.

I was standing there like an idiot, wearing my same old grubby clothes. Dean stood there looking like a model in a beautiful, pressed shirt and tie. He was taking me out. Not just out but *out.*

Some fancy place where you can't wear jeans.

I wanted to slide onto the floor. I had managed to ruin the date before it even started. It hit me then: I was so far out of my league it wasn't even funny.

I almost fainted with relief when Charisse piped up from across the room.

"I got this. She'll be down in five."

Dean looked both relieved and embarrassed as he turned and headed outside. Not nearly as embarrassed as *me* though. I felt like a natural-born moron.

"How'd you score that guy? He's ridic hot."

"I met him at work study."

"*He* does work study?"

I had stood stock still as Charisse held up various dresses in front of me. I was dazed. Thankfully, she was in her element.

Char loved fashion. I knew she was just playing dress up, and treating me like a doll. But at the moment, I didn't much care.

"No, he's on the football team. I work in the kitchen at the athletic department."

Charisse had stopped and lowered her arms. She stared at me in awe.

"You met him serving food in the caf?"

"Yes."

"You're joking."

I just shook my head. It was mostly the truth. That *was* where we met for the first time.

In person, anyway.

"You do realize that you sound like freaking Cinderella, right?"

I rolled my eyes, trying not to laugh. Charisse did kind of have a point... Dean was pretty much the Prince Charming type to a T. And I was definitely not prepared to go to the ball.

Not without help anyway.

I stepped into the purple and pink cocktail dress that Charisse held open for me. Then I sat still while my fairy godmother/roommate applied a thin layer of eyeshadow and powdered my nose. She handed me a pair of kitten heel pumps.

I slid them on and stood while Charisse looked me over, surveying her handiwork.

"Well, I have to admit you do clean up nice. Prince Charming won't know what hit him."

"He's not—"

"I know, I know. Just go — and be home before midnight."

Charisse winked knowingly. I giggled, rolling my eyes. But I hadn't left without hugging my friend.

"Thanks Charisse. I owe you one."

"Ain't that the truth. Now get!"

I walked uncertainly down the hallway in the heels as people stopped and stared at me. Thankfully the heels were relatively low, because otherwise I would have fallen on my behind.

I'd never worn anything higher than a sneaker in my life.

It was all worth it for the look on Dean's face though.

He looked awestruck for at least thirty seconds. Maybe longer. And then something shifted in his eyes. After that he'd looked hungry. Like he wanted to devour me.

"Wow, Krista... you look beautiful."

I swallowed nervously and lifted my chin. Fake it till you make it. That's what Nan always said.

So I did.

"Let's go."

CHAPTER 19

DEAN

I blinked, staring at the vision in front of me.

I still couldn't believe that she was the same girl. A dress, a little makeup, heels and KAPOW — she was gorgeous. Hotter than hot. A woman who could stop traffic.

To be honest, I felt almost like I'd been tricked. But I was 100% okay with it.

Krista wasn't just a sweet and pretty little thing as I'd previously thought she was.

She was stunning.

Movie star stunning.

In fact, I was having a little bit of trouble focusing on what she was saying. Something about being raised by her Grandmother, something about being here on scholarship, something about wanting to work in a museum restoring art. That's why she was majoring in art history and minoring in fine art.

She was fascinating. I cared about all those things. Of course I did. Her mind. Her soul. Her lips.

Especially her lips.

All I really wanted to do at the moment was kiss her.

"What about you?"

I forced myself to pay attention. She was staring at me inquisitively. I cleared my throat.

"Yes?"

"What about you? I don't know anything about you."

"Right. So, life story, the Cliff Notes version?"

She laughed. The sound was amazing. Like tinkling bells, but softer. I felt a shot of warmth go right to the pit of my stomach.

"If you like."

Krista leaned forward and placed her chin on her hands. I couldn't help but chuckle. She'd put me on the spot and wasn't being shy about it.

"Alright."

She took a sip and leaned forward again, her head tilted slightly to the side. I stared at her long graceful neck. I had a sudden urge to bite it.

Hard.

Yeah, no eating your date Dean. No matter how cute she is.

"I'm from New England — you knew that already — but I didn't tell you that my great-great-great-great-Grandfather is the one who founded our town. It's actually named after us. Westenville."

"Ooooh fancy. Go on."

I grinned at her self-consciously. I never felt particularly proud about my background, but it was a bit weird talking about it this way. I knew she didn't come from a family like mine.

But if she wanted to know, I'd tell her. I would do anything this girl asked of me.

Like, eat glass. Or walk through fire. Or sleep on a bed of nails.

No joke, I knew that I would do it. No questions asked. And no whining either.

It was strange, but true.

"Okay, here's something spooky. Each generation of my family has only given birth to one son. Supposedly it goes

71

back hundreds of years. But we all seem to live to be, um, unusually old."

"That's… really weird."

Krista had an odd look on her face. She looked a bit spooked — which after everything that had already happened was more than a bit disconcerting. If knowing each other from the dream world hadn't spooked her, why would this?

"What is?"

She took a deep breath and lifted her eyes to mine.

"In my family only one girl is born. They usually live a long life. Except for my mother, I guess. She, um…"

She trailed off, looking distressed. I hastened to put her at ease again, as quickly as possible. I was still afraid she would run out on me.

I didn't want our mutually weird families to mess up this date.

"It's okay. We don't have to talk about it."

She shook her head, as if dispelling the unpleasant thoughts inside.

"No, it's okay. She disappeared when I was seven. We don't know what happened to her to this day. She wouldn't just run off though. She loved us. Nan and me. We tried to find her, even hired a private detective after the police stopped looking. But we never found a trace."

Her eyes were shining with the force of her emotions. I'd never seen anything so beautiful in my life. Or felt someone else's sadness as keenly.

"I like to think… that's she's out there somewhere. Trying to find her way back to us."

My eyes were wide as I stared at her. Krista was so proud. Too proud to cry in front of me, even if it seemed like she might want to. She'd been through so much and was so strong. Brave too.

My life had been more than charmed compared to everything she'd told me.

The crazy part was I could tell she was just scratching the surface. Growing up as an orphan... with no idea what had happened to her one parent. It must have been so hard.

"I'm so sorry, Krista."

"Thank you. Anyway, she's not dead. I would know it if she was. But I can't find her when I'm— you know..."

"Dreamwalking."

"Yes! That's it exactly. Dreamwalking. I never called it that before, but it's perfect."

"What do you call it?"

She shrugged gracefully.

"Traveling I guess. Or just... going places. You have a special way with words, you know that? I'm not special like you."

I leaned across the table and took her hand.

"Yes, you are. Only you're even more special. I can barely do what you can do. Plus, you're much prettier."

She rolled her eyes and shook her head adamantly.

"All I can do is draw. I'm a hard worker and my grades always came easy. But that's it. Other than—"

I smiled at her. She was such a funny little thing. Didn't she know how incredible she was? She started fidgeting with her empty desert plate, self-conscious under my frank gaze.

Apparently not.

But I would be happy to show her.

In fact, I was going to make it my life's purpose.

I truly believed that. I did.

Right until the moment I fell asleep that night.

73

And then everything changed.

CHAPTER 20

KRISTA

*I*f this is a movie, I am the lonely girl who gets ghosted.

I hadn't seen Dean since our date. He hadn't called. He hadn't even taken any meals at the field house. At least, not when I was working.

I tilted my head, wondering if that was something he would do: find out when I was working somehow and stay away.

He was definitely avoiding me for some reason. And it hurt. It hurt me to the core.

But that wasn't even the worse part.

I hadn't even seen him in my dreams.

It had been over a week now. The only glimpse I'd gotten of Dean had been in English lit. And that hadn't exactly been romantic.

I'd spent the entire period excruciatingly aware of his nearness. Three times I'd nearly caught his eye. He'd been watching me surreptitiously but turned away the moment I'd looked.

Our eyes caught for a split-second before he looked away again.

For that brief moment though, the look in his eyes had been utterly bereft. No, devastated. He looked at me as if I'd done something wrong. Something to hurt him.

What the hell was going on with him?

I waited for him after class but he was gone. He must have snuck out through the fire exit. Yeah… he was that desperate to avoid me apparently.

That was just an extra dollop of humiliation on my banana split sundae of pain.

I had a terrible feeling in my chest. It was as if someone had reached inside me and put a block of ice inside, where my heart should be.

Snap out of it Krista. He dumped you. Get over it.

He didn't like me anymore. That was all. End of story. He was a rich gorgeous guy and I was… me.

I was just a mousy little girl who barely talked to anyone. There was nothing remarkable about me. Not like him. There was no reason for him to like me to begin with other than our odd connection.

And yet… he *had* liked me. A lot. I knew he had.

Something must have turned him off. My breath must have been bad, or my kisses had left him cold. It happened all the time. It was a simple story that happened every day all over the world and no reason to cry.

Boy meets girl. Girl gets dumped. The end.

Except, it wasn't just a simple story this time, and I knew it.

I worked yet another shift at the athletic center, working even harder than usual. I needed the distraction once I'd realized he wasn't going to show up. I volunteered to carry the heavy crates full of produce, stacking them in the cold room.

I kept hoping that if I worked hard enough, I'd wear myself out so I could sleep. Every night this week had been the same. I had barely gotten any rest. Just fitful sleep with no traveling and no visitors.

Even Charisse was starting to notice the bags under my eyes, silently handing me an eye mask and concealer this morning. We might not have anything in common other than gender, but Charisse wasn't the selfish brat she had seemed at first. She certainly had a soft spot for me, even if she called me a waif.

I walked back to my dorm, bones aching and miserable. But at least I was tired. I showered and climbed into bed, finally falling into an uneasy slumber.

That night when I slept, something different happened. Something bad. It was like someone else was in the dream with me. But not Dean.

Something dark.

For the first since I started dreamwalking, I couldn't control where I was going. The dream had me, not the other way around.

I screamed silence as I was dragged toward something. Or someone. Every instinct told me to fight it, to grab onto the earth beneath me, to hold on as hard as I could.

I woke up with a scream. It was still dark and I was sweating. I turned on the tiny clip on light I used to read or draw with when Charisse was sleeping.

I stared down at my hands. They were locked in a claw shape, like a crone or an animal's. I rubbed them, gingerly trying to bend and straighten them. It took a half hour before I could press my palms flat together.

I didn't go back to sleep. I just lay in the darkness, staring at the ceiling and praying for dawn.

I had been fighting something after all. But what? I'd never felt threatened in the dreams before. They were journeys, fun little trips full of curious exploration. And Dean.

My hands were sore for days.

CHAPTER 21

DEAN

I *was cursed.*

Every night since our date I had the dream. Every night, it was the same. I was alone, in a cold dark room. It was stone. Underground somewhere. Chains held me down, with shackles around my wrists and ankles.

No, they didn't just hold me.

They burned me.

I wish I could have said I was brave. That I knew I was dreaming and forced myself awake. That it wasn't real.

But it was.

And I was freaking *scared.*

I was there again, for the fifth night in a row. I twisted against my bonds, making them burn even more deeply into my flesh.

I opened my mouth to scream but a strange sound came from my throat. More like a roar than anything human. I sounded like a wild beast, trapped and frightened and angry. I sounded like an animal.

A big one.

Each morning I woke up exhausted, less rested than I'd been the night before. I would feel every ache and pain from the dream. They stayed with me.

So did the marks. Every morning, I woke with bruised and chafed skin on my wrists and ankles from where the chains had held me. Each morning, I watched as the marks slowly faded before my eyes.

I was tired and mentally exhausted but my body was stronger than ever. *Abnormally* strong. In fact, I felt like a freak of nature.

My reflexes were twice as fast. No, they were *ten times as fast.* And it was getting harder to hide the changes.

I knew what the guys were saying about me. That I juiced. That there was something wrong with me. Nobody should be that fast. That strong.

But I was.

I was a machine.

I thrived on the competition. Thrived on the game. I'd always loved sports but I'd never wanted to crush my opponents.

Now I did. Even during a practice skirmish. I went hell for leather against my own teammates.

But there was a problem. After practice, I had to eat. I had to risk seeing her or stay away. And then I'd have to go to sleep again. The urge to sleep came earlier each night. I'd be filled with dread as I fell into bed, profoundly exhausted, as if I could not stay awake another second.

As if the dream was claiming me, against my will.

And then the horror began again.

Every night, I'd hope for something new, for some relief from the pain. I'd hope to see *her.* But it was her fault somehow.

Krista had done this to me.

It was the same hell, every single night since the I'd kissed her lips. For the first time, I was dreamwalking without her. But somehow, she had started it all. It was her. I knew it was.

The same thing that drew me to her was the thing that I needed to stay away from.

I knew what I needed to do.

I needed to end it. To cut all ties. Sever the bond. Hide from her.

Then maybe I would go back to normal again.

It would be like cutting out a part of myself, but I had no choice. The hunger and aggression was too strong. It was tearing me apart. I was afraid I would hurt someone.

I was afraid I would hurt *her*.

For her own safety, I had to do something to stop it.

Otherwise I was afraid of what I might do.

The guys on the team were wrong. I wasn't turning into a machine. I was changing into a monster.

In the morning, I went to see her. I waited outside her dorm, staring up at the window that I somehow knew was hers. I could picture it clearly. The bed covered with the homespun quilt, the other side of the room an explosion of pink ruffles.

My beautiful girl huddled over a sketchpad.

Before I even texted, her face had appeared in the window. It was as if she'd sensed me. It shouldn't surprise me.

Nothing should surprise me anymore. But it did. The shot of hunger when I saw her face overwhelmed me.

I wanted her. And I wanted her to be mine. For good.

My stomach clenched with anxiety and longing. Another minute and she was downstairs, her face still soft and vulnerable from sleep.

Even now, knowing what I had to do, I wanted nothing more than to pull her into my arms and hold her. Tell her everything was going to be okay. That I would never leave her.

But it would be a lie.

I balled my hands into fists, shoving them deep into my pockets.

Just… get it over with, man.

"Hey," I said.

"Hey. Are you… alright?"

I just stared at her. I wanted to memorize her face. I wanted to make sure I never forgot the girl that shouldn't have been real but was.

"Not really."

"I haven't seen you lately." She shuffled her feet and I looked down, seeing the worn in penny loafers on her feet. "Did I do something wrong?"

Her face was vulnerable as she chewed her full bottom lip. I felt disgusted with myself for not being stronger. If I tried harder — maybe I could resist the violent urges. Maybe I could avoid hurting her.

But that was a lie. I had fought with everything I had. Nothing would slow the dangerous feelings inside me.

Except this.

I shook my head vehemently. Then I sighed.

"No, it's not you. But you were right. There is something wrong."

"Wrong?"

"There's something too risky about us being together. I wish I could explain it. You feel it too, don't you?"

Her mouth dropped open in surprise. For a moment, I thought she would argue with me. Fight me. I hoped she would.

She would tell me we would face this together. She would tell me she wanted to be with me — even if I was a monster. She would take me in her arms and kiss me, telling me she would never let me go.

She nodded and my heart sank. I'd wanted her to reason with me, to tell me it didn't matter, that we would find a solution together.

Instead she just nodded and gave me a sad smile.

"Yes. I do know."

I swallowed, the reality crashing down on me. This was it. She was saying it was over.

"Goodbye Dean. And…"

"Yes?"

"Good luck."

I stared at her slender back as she walked away. I felt my heart crack open and everything inside me poured out. I was empty and alone.

But maybe, just maybe, I would be human again.

CHAPTER 22

KRISTA

The next few weeks passed in a blur. I went about my business woodenly, feeling strangely hollow inside. It was stupid to feel that way. I barely knew Dean. At least that's what I told myself again and again.

It didn't do a thing to ease the ache inside me.

I knew I had lost something precious. Dean had made me feel like I was something more than just a shy little girl. Without him, it felt like the other half of myself was gone.

I was being pathetic. He had moved on. I had to move on, too.

So I picked myself up and got on with it. I went to class. I went to work. I'd been waiting to go to college for what seemed like forever. I might as well make the most of it.

As usual, I excelled at my studies. I was expecting straight A's in all my classes. All except for Freshman Lit. I barely heard a word the professor said. I almost transferred out of the class, feeling foolish at the way my heart leapt every time I saw Dean there.

Even being in the room with him was enough to soothe me somehow, even though it made me feel twisted up inside. He was pretty much my own private heaven and hell, all at once.

Meanwhile, he ignored me completely.

I hadn't caught him looking at me again. I was certain I could feel his eyes on me sometimes. I noticed that Dean had dark shadows under his eyes as well. That was interesting.

His and hers matching eye bags.

How… romantic.

Of course, I was sure he had moved on, in the real sense of the word. I often saw girls trailing behind him after class or around the quad. They were always approaching him, almost glomming onto him.

But it didn't make me jealous. He didn't seem to respond with anything more than polite disinterest. I had a strange feeling that he hated it.

That, like me, he wanted to be left alone.

But there was no way to know if that was true, or if it was wishful thinking. We would have to actually talk to each other to do that, and we had both decided that was a terrible idea.

My ability to dreamwalk had returned, slowly at first. I felt tentative in a way I never had before. Almost like I was a stranger in the once familiar world of night. I stuck closer to home too, exploring the campus and city nearby.

I forced myself to stay away from Dean, even when my feet led me invariably towards the athletic housing complex. I felt his pull though. I was like a walking, talking compass.

A broken compass that always pointed 'due Dean.'

I knew he was out there, dreamwalking without me. His power seemed to have grown, even as my own diminished.

Or if not diminished, *changed.*

I shook my head, forcing myself to get back to work. It was mindless labor, which allowed my mind to wander. I was at the dining hall again, working yet another shift. I'd even switched my time slot, hoping to catch a glimpse of him. In case he was avoiding me… there was no way he would know that I would be there.

Oh yeah, I was definitely pathetic.

This weekend was going to be different though. I was going out. Charisse had made me promise to hit some parties. I dreaded it, but I'd already agreed in a moment of weakness.

I snorted. Who was I kidding? *All* of my moments felt like moments of weakness.

Social situations like that were my Achilles' heel.

I would just have to grin and bear it. Besides, I owed Charisse. She'd done so much for me over the past month, even making me bingewatch Netflix with her to cheer me up.

So, I would go and try not to look too miserable.

It wouldn't be easy, but I was getting better at it. I could just pretend I was back in high school, and pin a smile on my face. Though the truth was, I had never even gone to a keg party back home. Not one.

Just blend in. Hide in plain sight.

Be invisible.

Fade away.

CHAPTER 23

DEAN

I dreamed about her that night. That was nothing new. I felt like I'd spent half my life dreaming about her.

But this time it was different. This time I had a purpose, and as soon as I knew I was in the dream, I did something I'd never dared to do before.

This time I went to her.

Like the other dreams, I was lucid. I didn't wake up in chains. I woke in my own bed, in the athlete housing complex. Before I knew it, I was outside, walking through campus.

Well, 'walking' was relative.

My steps were so broad that each one traversed fifteen feet or more. I felt strong, invincible even. I felt like I was somehow *more than.*

Something bigger than myself. Stronger. Braver.

And I was searching for the one person who would see it.

I might be cursed, but Krista knew me. She would understand. I hoped she would anyway.

My feet carried me inevitably toward her dorm. I didn't even have to think about which way to go. She drew me, almost as if she was a magnet. As if I were an animal on the hunt who had caught her scent. But not to kill her.

To be with her.

It was more than just an animal attraction. I felt driven to be as close to her as possible. To combine with her, on a spiritual level. To conjoin.

To absorb and be absorbed.

I stared up to a window on the third floor, sensing that she was inside. I blinked and I was inside her room, staring down at her delicate body, twisted in a homemade quilt.

I wondered briefly if dream sex would be as fun as real sex. Or even more fun.

Either way, I was definitely wanting to crawl into that bed with her. Not until she was aware of my presence though. I already felt a bit like a creeper.

A dreamcreeper. Nice, Dean.

I smiled tenderly at the picture she made. She slept in the same white nightgown that I remembered from before. She looked delicious, her face softened in sleep, her long legs tangled up in her mismatched sheets.

This time it was me who reached out and pressed my hand against her chest.

Immediately her eyes opened, looking adorably surprised. She wasn't frightened though. She smiled when she saw who it was.

"I missed you."

"I missed you, too."

I took her hand and pulled her into my arms. She felt warm and soft and alluring as hell. I brushed her hair back and kissed her.

Her soft lips parted underneath mine. I pulled her even closer, my arms holding her tightly against me.

She kissed me back, then pulled away. She looked worried. I didn't want to let her out of my arms.

"Let me kiss you. I'm sorry. For everything."

"It's not that."

"What then?"

"I have to tell you something, Dean. Something I never seem to remember when I wake up."

"What?"

"They're after—"

In an instant I was back in my own bed, covered in sweat. Her cut off words started to fade from my memory. I could remember almost every other detail about the dream, from the warm feeling of her skin underneath my palm, to the lack of decorations on her side of her dorm room, to the feeling of the cool night air on my skin as I travelled across the campus.

I also understood something new.

The feeling I had in the dream was still with me, but stronger than before.

Touching her in the dream had changed me. Again. It felt like another door had been unlocked inside me, and God only knew what was rushing through.

Raw power. Anger. Need.

I felt powerful, more alive than ever before. I felt something inside me surging. Heat, vitality, desire.

At practice that morning, I was unstoppable. I ran circles around my teammates until they started to look at me differently. I saw fear and respect in their eyes. Coach pulled me aside and said that if I kept it up, I'd be starting.

The first Freshman starting quarterback in the league.

Ever.

Old Dean would have been thrilled. Honored. Humbled.

But new Dean wasn't like that. I just took it as my due. I knew without a doubt that I deserved it. The new Dean wasn't just top dog. I was *the* top dog.

I was the Alpha.

CHAPTER 24

KRISTA

"E*xcuse me.*"

I scooted backwards as a group of girls moved past me down the hallway. I watched them go, feeling like I was on a nature special. The girls at this party all seemed to move in packs, like wild dogs.

Pedigreed dogs with diamond collars and chips embedded under their sleek fur.

Speaking of dogs… a group of guys in backward baseball caps seemed to trail after the girls. I overheard a few of the things they were saying. Mostly the word 'hot' and 'ass.' One of them said he wanted to 'git some.'

Ew.

So this was a frat party.

What the heck was I doing here again?

I sighed, staring at the rows of blonde girls that seemed to line the walls. I felt more out of place than ever. Apparently, Charisse was thinking about joining a sorority, and this was an open invitational.

The girl who had greeted us at the door had explained it all, making it seem like we were lucky to be there. Usually it was Greeks only. I sipped my tepid beer and resisted the urge to roll my eyes.

'Open invitational' apparently meant bad beer and a vile punch that I wouldn't even get close to. This wasn't a party. It was my worst nightmare.

Charisse on the other hand seemed to be entirely in her element. She was smiling and laughing, making friends so quickly it made my head spin. My roommate knew this world and wanted to be part of it. Even if that meant dragging *me* along with her.

Apparently, I was her wing-woman.

She'd even dressed me up. Charisse gave me a pair of stretch jeans that she said she couldn't fill out well enough. A ruffly silk top in dark green completed the look.

The whole outfit was a gift, just cast off clothes that Charisse thought would look better on me. She said it like it was no big deal. As if designer clothes grew on trees.

Who knows? Maybe in Charisse's world, they did.

To be honest, I was not sure what to make of my roommate most of the time.

Charisse was superficial and overly concerned with fitting in, but she was also smart as a whip. She got good grades seemingly without trying. And she seemed to know everything about everything.

She was exceedingly generous with me, doling out clothes and makeup and unsolicited advice left and right. She had made it her personal mission to draw me out of my shell.

The crazy part was that I didn't mind. I even appreciated it. I knew Charisse meant well and had a big heart, despite my first impressions.

But Charisse was also part of this world, and it was time for me to make my exit. There was no point in staying here and torturing myself. My roomie was fine.

My wing-woman duties had been fulfilled.

I knew I would never be comfortable here, no matter how much flat beer I drank. Everyone either stared at me or ignored me completely, as if I were a part of the wallpaper.

Speaking of which…

Two frat guys who had been staring at me came over with a six pack of imported beer. One of them was pretty cute. His friend was tall and thin and gawkish. The cute one wore a baseball cap, facing forward thankfully.

I reminded myself not to judge people based on appearance. After all, I hated it when people did that to me.

And they always did.

"Hey, you look lonely over here all by yourself."

I raised an eyebrow.

"You mean out of place?"

They were staring at me like I was a bug on the wall. I was about to excuse myself when I caught my roommate smiling and giving me a thumbs up. I sighed, finally realizing what the term 'taking one for the team' meant.

Besides, I really shouldn't leave her here alone. Not to mention the text messages I was trying to ignore that had been showing up all day. Dean had decided to talk to me again, just like that.

Well, I wasn't having it.

The cute one offered me a beer and I took it, removing the top myself. I wasn't stupid. Bottled beer was safer at a college party. It was smart to keep an eye on your own drink, and your friend's. All the time.

Everyone knew that.

Baseball cap guy looked a little dazed as he leaned against the wall.

"No, man. You're gorgeous."

The other guy nodded, still staring at me.

"Yeah man. Different."

I cringed. That was the one word that people always used to describe me. For once I would like someone to call me 'smart' or even 'pretty' without qualifying it.

I.e. 'You seem pretty smart for a hick.'

"I'm a typical college freshman. Not exactly exotic."

"Yeah. Cool."

He nodded at me like an idiot but the cute one wasn't as stupid. Baseball cap guy elbowed him. Hard.

"Shut up Harry. You sound like an idiot."

He grinned at me, holding out his hand.

"I'm Luke. This is Harrison. Harrison, go get us some more beer."

Harrison did as he asked while Luke explained the frat hierarchy. Harrison was an underclassman. Luke was a senior. So he got to order him around.

Luke turned out to be smarter than he looked. Polite even. He sent Harrison to get a couple of folding chairs for us to sit in. He even took off his baseball cap, like a true gentleman.

I was well aware that I was getting hit on. But he wasn't trying to get me drunk or drag me off to his room. It seemed harmless, pleasant even.

So I let it happen. Why not, right?

Got to go with the flow, Krista.

Luke wasn't Dean. Not even close. But he was easier to talk to than I'd expected. And I was flattered by his obvious interest.

So when he offered me another beer I shrugged and said something I probably shouldn't have.

"Why not?"

CHAPTER 25

DEAN

here was she?

I'd been texting Krista since I got up. So far she hadn't responded. But I knew she had read them. It was stupid of her to ignore me like this.

She had no idea that she was poking a bear.

I sat at the kitchen table, eating my takeout wings and drinking a beer. Somehow there was always beer in the fridge. It seemed like I was always drinking lately. And eating. I seemed to burn through the calories twice as fast as before.

New Dean needed more fuel. Plus, if I got drunk enough, maybe I could sleep deeply. Maybe I would not dream.

'Dream.' What a joke. What a safe, nice little word. And so far from the truth.

I hadn't dreamwalked in days. Now every night I spent hours being torn apart and put back together as someone else.

Some*thing* else.

Dream was too nice a word for what had been happening lately. I'd been having increasingly horrific nightmares.

I was lucid for every torturous moment of the transformation that came over me. My bones lengthening, my skin changing, my mouth morphing forward into the shape of an animal's muzzle lined with viciously sharp teeth.

My keen awareness that only one person could help me. The one person who I'd chased away.

And I was too afraid she might never take me back.

"Come on man, let's go out. My bro is having a party."

I shrugged and pushed my food away, following Chuck out of the suite. I had been avoiding the guys and the party atmosphere. Tonight, it was quiet though.

Everyone had found someplace else to get their jollies.

It probably had something to do with me. I hadn't said a word. But they could tell I wanted to tear their heads off. Not metaphorically.

Literally.

But a party? Why the hell not. Just another place to get drunk. To blot out the painful reality that was tearing me apart.

It was starting to rain as we walked through campus to the row of frat houses just beyond. Random dudes were not welcome at these parties, but as athletes, we were invited just about everywhere.

I stood outside the house with my beer, letting the water soak me to the bone.

"Your beer is getting watery."

A cute redhead was smiling at me, ignoring the fact that her top was getting wet.

Actually, maybe that was deliberate.

"Come inside, silly. I'll help you get dry."

I brushed by her, and went inside the crowded frat house. I ignored the redhead who was sticking to me like static cling. I grabbed a bottle of booze off the bar and started drinking straight from it.

No one complained. Even if they had, I didn't care. Nothing mattered. I was numb to it all.

Until I saw her.

I stood there, dripping water all over the floor. I could hardly believe my eyes.

She was here.

Krista was here.

I'd been worried about her, thinking she was sad and angry. Thinking she missed me. But no. She was at a freaking frat party.

Getting hit on, no less.

Krista was sitting in a lawn chair on the landing halfway up the stairs. She was laughing at something a bro with wavy blond hair was saying to her. She was lit up, looking even prettier than usual, which was saying a lot.

The flirtatious look on her face was like a knife in my gut.

I knew, I *knew* that she had every right to move on. I'd been the one who started the conversation that ended things. But that was a rational voice. My other voice was much, *much* louder.

The voice that spoke in grunts and growls.

That voice wanted to tear this guy's throat out.

I was across the room and up the stairs in two shakes, staring down at them.

"What are you doing here?"

She looked surprised to see me at first. Almost happy. Then her expression changed to one of hurt. In a split second, her face had shuttered.

Closed for business.

At least, for me.

Yeah, I'd blown it with her. Maybe for good. But that didn't mean I was going to let some swine take a crack at her.

Not on my watch.

I stepped closer, until my knees were practically touching hers.

"You don't belong here, Krista."

She wouldn't look at me. She looked embarrassed. I hated seeing her look upset. But it was even worse to see her trying to disappear into her lifted shoulders. She looked *humiliated.*

Dammit.

The imbecile next to her stood up.

"Hey man, back off. She's my guest."

I didn't recognize my own voice as I turned to face the guy. I was filled with visions of him touching her. Kissing her.

More.

"Did you touch her?"

The guy looked taken aback by my tone of voice. Then he stood up straighter like he thought he stood a chance. All frat boy swagger.

Oh boy did he have another thing coming.

"You need to back off, man."

I stepped closer until we were almost chest to chest. He flinched. I didn't.

"Says who?"

"My name is Luke and I live here. Who the hell are you?"

People were gathering around us, eager for a fight. Chuck tried to step between us, but I shouldered him away. I wanted to fight. I wanted to do more than that.

The darkness inside me threatened to spill over and swallow me up.

"Come on Dean, it's not worth it. Plenty of fish in the sea, remember?"

"It? You mean 'her.' She's a freaking human being. And she's mine."

Chuck shut up when he saw the look on my face. I knew I was snarling. I had a very, very thin hold on my self-control. I had a feeling it was about to snap.

"Hey man, it's a free country. She can talk to whoever she wants to."

The idiot actually grinned at me. Like this was a game.

"And she wants to talk to me."

Even Krista tried to talk some sense into the guy.

"Luke, don't. I'll go. Okay, Dean?"

I gave her a dark look and she paled. I was breathing heavily, trying to decide if I should throw the little pissant down the stairs or just choke him where he stood. I remembered the way Krista had smiled at Luke and the decision was made.

Choking. Definitely choking.

I reached out and grabbed Luke's throat, lifting him off his feet. People tried to pull my hands away but I was too strong. It was like dusting ants off a blanket at a picnic.

Easier.

I snarled at the surprised look on the frat boy's face. He clawed at my hand on his throat. Everyone was shouting at once. Chuck was screaming into my ear but I barely heard him.

"Come on man, you are going to get benched for fighting."

"Does it look like I'm fighting?"

I wasn't, I was just taking out the trash. I was on the verge of tossing him across the landing when I felt it.

A soft hand on my shoulder. Her voice penetrated the haze of red over my vision. I felt a strange calmness settle over me, washing away the unchecked rage.

"Put him down Dean."

Like a trained doggy, I did.

CHAPTER 26

KRISTA

Thump thump thump thump thump

My heart was pounding so hard it felt like it might fly out of my chest.

It was over in two seconds. Luke wasn't ever in any real danger. He'd simply rubbed his throat and walked away.

A few minutes more though... Luke might have ended up in the hospital. Or worse.

Dean had almost killed him.

I pushed the thought aside. Dean wasn't like that. I knew him. He wouldn't hurt a fly.

Dean was harmless.

Even as I thought the words I knew it was a lie.

The old Dean would not have hurt a fly. The new Dean was something else entirely. Brooding. Aggressive. Lost.

He was just... different.

Dean's friend Chuck was smoothing things over so no charges would be pressed.

I was shocked by the violence that had come from Dean in those few moments. He wasn't himself. And when he looked at me, he had looked almost as surprised as I was.

Almost like he was afraid of his own strength. And he was strong. Unnaturally strong.

No human being could lift an adult man with one hand like that. And he hadn't even broken a sweat.

He let go immediately when I touched him. He just stood there, staring me. Our eyes locked for a heartbeat. Then he sneered and grabbed my arm, pulling me down the stairs and out into the rain. I was running just to keep up with him.

"Dean—"

I tried to lean back and dig my heels in but it didn't even slow him.

"Dean! Stop! You're pulling me too hard!"

I stumbled as he stopped abruptly, turning to face me.

"Are you injured?"

I rubbed my arm gingerly. It was fine. He hadn't hurt me, just startled me.

Well, that was putting it mildly.

"No. I'm okay."

He ran his hand through his hair, staring at me with a dark look.

"I don't want to hurt you. I don't care about anyone else — just not you."

"I know."

"Tell me the truth then. Is that your new boyfriend? Did you hook up with him, Krista? Did you?"

He held my shoulders, not quite shaking me, though it seemed like he wanted to. His touch was gentle somehow, despite the desperate anger in his face. I realized I could have broken free easily. But I was too stunned to step away.

"No, I just met him. I swear."

"Don't lie to me! I've been going out of my head, and you just moved on. Admit it!"

"Nothing is going on Dean! Not that it's any of your freaking business."

His arms dropped. He looked hurt for a minute. Almost like I'd slapped him. Then he stepped in, so close he was almost touching me. I could smell the alcohol on his breath as it fanned my face.

Great. Robo-Dean was drunk.

"But that's not really true is it, Krista? You know that it *is* my business. Everything about you is my business."

He ran his fingertips over my cheek. We were both getting soaked as the rain started again in earnest.

"Whether either one of us wants it to be or not."

His fingers ran down to my chin. He gripped it, forcing me to look him in the eyes.

"Luckily for me, I'm happy to make you my business. Permanently."

He let go abruptly and turned, walking briskly towards campus. I stood in the rain, shivering and alone.

"Are you coming?"

I just stared at him, shocked by his admission.

He stopped and came back, taking my hand. He stared at my palm as he ran his thumb over the sensitive skin.

I shivered again, but not because I was cold.

Dean was such a contradictory combination of rough and tender. He had been acting like a lunatic less than ten minutes ago. His voice was husky as he murmured to me.

"Come on, you need to get out of the rain. I don't want you to get sick."

I said nothing. I let him lead me back towards my dorm. He opened the door and I stepped inside, just out of the rain. He stayed outside, letting the water pour down his face.

He looked so lost and alone in that moment, I had to stop myself from reaching out to him.

"What about you? Don't you have a big game coming up or something?"

He laughed, the sound surprisingly bitter. He held out his arms, letting the rain drench every inch of him. Then he tilted his head back and opened his mouth, drinking it in. He looked wild somehow.

Wild and untamed. Dangerous.

His blue eyes were practically glowing as he lowered his face, staring at me hard.

"Look at me. I don't get sick, Krista."

Then he stepped forward and kissed my mouth, hard and fast. I gasped at the suddenness of it. The heat.

Then he turned and ran off into the rain. So fast, he disappeared into the gray night before I knew it.

Just like that, he was gone.

CHAPTER 27

DEAN

It was official.

I was going to hell.

I'd almost hurt her. In that moment, when I'd looked at Krista, I'd seen something to devour. Just for a split second, but it had been there.

Eat. Bite. Tear.

My conscience had reared up almost as quickly, telling me no.

Not her. *Never* her.

The horror of my ravenous hunger terrified me. I had to get away before I did something terrible. I had to get as far as I could from the source of all of it.

Krista.

I ran through campus, not returning to the athlete housing. I ran past the neat rows of townhouses and straight into the woods. I only stopped when I was miles from campus, out of breath, bent over and heaving.

I had never run that fast in my life, or been more afraid. Nothing scared Dean Westen. Why should it? My life had been charmed.

The strangest thing was, I had a feeling that was about to change. Had already changed. I was doomed, from the moment I met her.

I wiped my lips on my sleeve. My arm came away wet. The rain had stopped at least twenty minutes ago so it wasn't water. It looked like I'd been drooling.

Jesus Dean, one kiss from a pretty girl and you start drooling?

I wanted to laugh at the joke, the idea was so ridiculous. But for some reason it just wasn't funny.

It wasn't funny at all.

In fact, at that moment, it was probably the least funny thing I'd heard in my life.

It took me over an hour to walk back to the edge of campus through the woods. I'd gone even further than I'd realized in my inhuman burst of speed.

Even my roommates were in bed by the time I crawled under the covers. I didn't shower, preferring to have the scent of the forest with me.

The woods had been so quiet and peaceful. There was no one to accidentally hurt, or call me a monster. And yet there was something wild and untamed about the deep, dark woods. Something that reminded me of what I was becoming.

That night, when I dreamed, I returned there.

CHAPTER 28

KRISTA

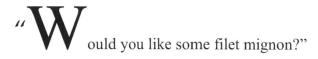"ould you like some filet mignon?"

"Yes."

I cut open the haunch of beef, watching as the juices ran freely to the cutting board. I placed a thick slice on the plate in front of me without lifting my eyes.

I could feel him there, staring at me. I recognized his voice and felt the pull to smile at him, talk to him. But I resisted.

I glanced up in time to see Dean turn away.

This was my fault. I should have asked for a different shift, a different service.

I could have asked to stay in the back. I *should* have. But I was too weak.

I couldn't help but want to see him, even if it was just across the lecture hall on Wednesdays. Or the dining hall every Monday and Thursday. Nothing had changed in that way. I still craved his nearness.

He was the one who had been stoically ignoring me for weeks now.

Until the party.

He'd been drunk. And dangerously angry. He'd gotten territorial over me. That was all it was, right?

I half-expected him to begin ignoring me again. If I was smart, I would hope that he would. Apparently, I wasn't that smart.

I had been ready to tell him to go to hell when he'd dragged me out of that frat house. I might be small, but nobody told me what to do.

But then I'd seen the look in his eyes. Desperate and lonely. It echoed the way I always felt but never shared. And he'd let *me* see it.

So I kept my head down and worked, stealing an occasional glance at Dean.

When I looked up he was staring at me, a haunted look in his eyes. His gaze was traveling over my neck and throat, down to my chest and lower. I was wearing an apron so he couldn't really check me out.

But Dean was making his best effort.

I gasped at the look on his face. I dropped the serving fork and took a step back at the blatant lust in his eyes. It was as if he could see through my clothes. I blushed bright red, feeling naked and exposed.

"Krista, do you need a break?"

Pam checked up on me now and then. She walked the floor, keeping her eye on everything. She ran a tight kitchen. She was a good boss. She didn't make them work crazy hard, but she didn't allow for slacking either.

She would definitely notice one of her servers standing like an idiot in the middle of the floor.

I shook myself, waking up from the trance Dean had put me in. I glanced at my boss, embarrassed.

"No, I'm fine."

Pam smiled at me, lifting an eyebrow.

"You sure?"

I nodded, feeling the red travel to the back of my neck. I could *feel* him staring at me. Still.

"Then get back to it."

I nodded my head dumbly and stepped back to my station.

Another group of players had just come in. I served them one at a time, trying to ignore the feeling of Dean's eyes on me.

When I looked up again, he was smiling humorlessly, rubbing his thumb across his lips as he stared at my mouth. I gasped, shocked at the sudden feeling that he was actually touching me, not just looking.

He lifted his eyes to mine. They were cold and hard but somehow full of fire. I swallowed, forcing myself to look away. I knew my cheeks were burning.

Dean Westen had a habit of making me blush.

Dean didn't leave until the dining hall closed that night, or the next two nights I worked. In fact, he did the same thing in English class. And then he followed me home.

But he never approached me or said a word

He just... watched me. And he waited. What he was waiting for, I wasn't sure. Maybe he knew I was mad at him. Maybe he was waiting for an invitation.

Well, I hoped he liked disappointment because it would be a cold day in hell before I took him back.

I wasn't sure exactly how I felt, to be honest.

On one hand, I missed him. I still felt goosebumps and butterflies around him. But I didn't like the way he was acting.

The new Dean was way too alpha. The way he circled around me was exactly like an animal, marking his territory. It was insulting and reassuring at the same time.

But I also felt hunted, as if I were a small prey animal and he was a ferocious killer.

Not that I feared him exactly. It was more that I feared myself. Whatever it was inside me that leapt up to answer him.

It was a cruel joke.

I'd wanted desperately to see him again. Now it seemed that he had decided to stop fighting whatever drew us together. But he didn't approach me. He just watched and waited.

That's when the dreams started in earnest again.

Along with a bunch of other weird stuff.

CHAPTER 29

DEAN

Running.

I was running. Tall grass brushed my belly as I raced through the soft sand. I knew exactly where I was. The dunes near my family's house.

The dunes that led to the water. I'd been here a hundred times.

A thousand.

But everything looked odd. The perspective was wrong. The angles of the earth and sky. It took me a while to figure out what it was.

When I did, I was horrified.

I was too low to the ground, running like an animal on all fours. I wasn't a man anymore.

I was a beast.

Once I understood though, I moved faster. My limbs ate the ground as they moved in tandem. It was so easy, like second nature to me. Even though I'd never run on all fours before.

Something pulled me forward, despite my feeling of unease. I raced up the coast, traveling at an astounding rate. The scenery blurred past me as I picked up speed.

I stopped, realizing I was somewhere else. Someplace unfamiliar.

I crossed a thin barrier of sand. A stretch of land too narrow for buildings or roads. Then I was there.

Whatever had been drawing me was close. I could feel it. A rocky, impenetrable coast spread out before me. It ran in a circle, surrounding the small island completely.

Somewhere in the back of my mind I heard a voice whisper a name.

Darkstar.

A huge stone building stood at the pinnacle of the island, almost like an ancient fortress. It loomed, almost as if it was alive. As if the structure *itself* had bad intentions.

Something resonated inside me when I saw it. Recognition. Fear. Anger.

I knew this place.

In the dream I began to climb the rocks, full of fear and longing in equal measures. I had to get inside. It was the most important thing I could imagine. I was instantly obsessed, like I had been with Krista.

It was need that devoured me from inside.

I tried to grasp at the loose rocks that led up the cliff but my hands were clumsy and oddly shaped. I looked down on myself and saw something that frightened me to the core.

My hands — if you could call them that — the grotesquely misshapen hands ended in sharp talons. But that wasn't the worst part. My skin was covered in fur.

I woke up covered in sweat and shaking from exertion. I cleaned myself up and changed my damp sheets. I lay on top of the covers as dawn lit up the sky.

I didn't sleep. I wasn't prepared to face the dreams again.

But I did come to a decision.

Something was happening to me. Something connected to Krista. I was used to the idea already. But now I had a glimpse of what I was becoming.

A monster.

110

I was done fighting whatever this was. It was pointless anyway. Whatever I was becoming, I knew it was too late to go back. I had already changed far too much.

And whatever role Krista played in it... well I was done fighting that too.

The time had come to claim her as my own.

CHAPTER 30

KRISTA

*T*he butterflies were back.

Not in my stomach, but the real ones. Small purple ones that seemed to follow me wherever I went. I hadn't seen them much lately, not since two summers ago, but I knew what it meant.

Even though I was still angry at Dean, even though I felt lost, I was happy.

Because he hadn't given up on me.

A strange energy coursed through me as I doled out cocktails in one of the private boxes at the stadium. It was yet another fundraising event for high rollers. But for once, I wasn't intimidated.

I stood up straighter, moved faster. My body was thrumming with barely restrained power and an eagerness to unleash it.

It wasn't my own power, but I felt it. And I knew where it came from.

It was *his*.

Dean was down there somewhere, getting ready to take the field. It was weird being here, watching him play, when we still hadn't spoken since that night. Not with words anyway.

But we both knew, there would be words. Lots of them. Soon. The silence wasn't stopping anything that was happening. It was just making both of us miserable.

We had to talk.

Tonight, in fact.

In the meantime, I had VIPs to tend to.

I bustled around, serving food and drinks in one of the skyboxes, the super expensive seats that were high up in the center of the stadium. The views were ideal, not too close that you were on the field, but high enough that you could see the action on long plays and field goal kicks.

The best part of the deal in my opinion was that the boxes were temperature controlled. While the players and fans were out there sweating or freezing, important donors and guests of the university were in here, cool or cozy, depending on the season.

There were little TVs scattered around the room for close ups of the action. There was a private, fully stocked top-shelf bar with gourmet food service. They even had special uniforms for the servers.

I was wearing a starched white uniform with team color accents and a cute little apron with a pocket for tips. They hadn't even made me wear a hairnet, just a jaunty little white paper cap.

It looked kind of silly, but I pinned it in place without a word of complaint. I was excited. I couldn't help it.

I wanted to be here for Dean. Watch him play. Maybe even cheer a little if he scored.

I didn't really mind looking silly anyway. I was just excited to watch the game. It was my first time working at the stadium, or coming to a game. Though the truth was, I'd known how well Dean was doing in the first few games of the season.

I couldn't help it. Even if I hadn't read the news articles, it was hard to avoid the topic of the new star player.

Dean was a sensation here. There was no doubt, he was going places. Maybe even all the way to the pros.

Plus, the gig gave me time to think about what I would do *afterwards*.

About Dean.

Forgive him? Or try and forget him?

Both had seemed impossible before today.

Everything had changed. After two weeks of longing looks and radio silence, he'd finally broken the heavy tension between us. Dean had texted me this morning to meet him after the game.

He hadn't asked me. He'd informed me of his plans. Whatever he was wrestling with, it had shifted somehow.

The way he'd been watching me the past few weeks... well, he scared me a little.

I didn't think he'd hurt me, but there was something dangerous about him now. Not just what had happened at the frat party either.

How could he have changed that quickly though? It didn't make any sense. Not logical sense anyway.

If you believed in magic though… well, it was more than possible.

For some reason, I still trusted him. I had immediately. Almost from the moment we'd met.

Well… dream-Krista had trusted dream-Dean.

Even if we hadn't spoken during the day, we'd been together almost every night this week. Lately, he'd been taking charge of our excursions… brimming with energy. Coming to my room. Taking me on long dreamwalks up the coast.

At some point in the dream, his eyes would change. And he would disappear, racing ahead of me. So far and so fast I could never hope to catch up.

He was trying to show me something, I just didn't quite know what it was yet.

All I knew was I didn't want to lose him. I was painfully aware of his presence in the stadium, even 500 feet from the box. We were connected, for better or worse.

Maybe even forever.

I sighed, wishing my mother were here. Or even back home, where I could call her. I needed talk to her, badly.

Yeah, I wanted my mommy. Didn't matter that she'd been gone for a decade. I needed her just as badly as I had when I was a little girl.

Maybe even more.

Nan didn't really understand modern boys, and there had never been anything to talk about. Not until Dean. I couldn't tell Charisse because of the unusual nature of my relationship with Dean, whatever it was.

This didn't count as ordinary, everyday boy troubles, that was for sure.

Somehow though, I felt sure my mother would have understood. She'd dreamt too. Maybe it was even hereditary. Sometimes I thought... maybe she had left to protect me somehow.

It was probably just wishful thinking, but it felt right.

It felt true.

I served another gin and tonic and a plate of spicy wings, shifting my eyes to the screen as Dean threw the ball in a high arc. He was incredible. He even looked larger than usual on the tiny screen as the game progressed.

I watched in awe as his strides took him through the line of scrimmage and further than any other player on the field. He shouldered them out of his way without visible effort. I blinked and he was already running into the end zone.

My mouth opened in surprise. *Goodness.* He was phenomenal. Unbelievably strong, and yet somehow graceful and precise. As if he'd been born to do this.

I shouldn't have been surprised. I knew he was talented. I just hadn't expected him to dominate the field, making the other players seem like children playing vainly against a giant.

My giant.

I spent the rest of the game with my gaze trained on his broad back, barely able to tear my eyes away to serve drinks.

CHAPTER 31

DEAN

*L*ook out suckers, daddy's home.

I ran past the former quarterback to take the starting position. Ryan glared at me, but even he had known it was inevitable. It was humiliating for a Senior to be replaced by a Freshman, but it didn't matter. I could play circles around the guy in my sleep.

Inevitable, like I said.

It was unheard of, to have a Freshman take over for a seasoned Senior. But I had been unstoppable in practice, even singlehandedly winning last week's game, a lost cause at halftime when they put me in.

So this time, I was starting.

I smiled confidently, ready to go to war. I was making national news tonight. But none of it mattered. Nothing mattered.

I grit my teeth and got into position.

Don't think about it.

Don't think about *her*.

Two weeks ago, when I'd seen her at the party, I'd finally given in to the truth. Krista belonged to me. I was going to make her my girlfriend, officially.

More than that, I was going to *keep* her.

I'd never once been tempted to mess around with other girls, not since the moment I knew she was real. I preferred to take out my frustrated desires on the field.

Thanks to my elusive soon-to-be girlfriend, I had a lot of frustration. Some of it was the change, and some was her.

I was getting stronger by the day, more vicious, more alpha. Nobody argued with me, or even approached me anymore.

Now they just followed. Looked away. Did what they were told.

During the day, I was invincible. Unstoppable. Unbreakable.

But not at night. When I was alone and the dreams came, I was worse than weak. I was vulnerable. Utterly helpless.

I wondered if it would be different with her beside me, wrapped in my arms while we slept. It might help, it might not. Maybe she knew a way to control it, or at least who *they* were and what they wanted from me.

Either way, I was not going to let her go.

Even if being with her increased the torment, instead of ending it.

I leaned forward and got into position.

My mind cleared in an instant.

My vision focused to the point where I could see the sweat dripping down the faces of the opposing team. I could see every fan in the stadium. I could see every blade of grass on the field.

I inhaled and waited for the second whistle.

The game began again.

CHAPTER 32

KRISTA

I rolled the mop down the sloped hallway to the service closet. I couldn't help but glance over my shoulder as I pushed the mop inside.

This place was creepy at night.

In fact, I had the distinct feeling I wasn't alone.

I cleared my throat and pulled off the rubber gloves, wiping my hands down the front of my uniform. The gloves made my hands mega sweaty. It was pretty gross.

Come on Krista, it's just an empty stadium.

I thought I might be feeling the energy of the place. So much happened here. The fans went through huge emotional swings.

Not to mention the three or four players that had been injured.

Yeah. Dean was kind of a steam roller out there tonight. He'd played well, but he was almost too rough.

Like he was enjoying hurting the opposing team.

And he had. There had been at least two stretchers carried off the field tonight. And that was just when I was looking.

I grabbed my bag from behind the bar and headed through the quiet hallways. I kept jumping, feeling like I was in danger. I brushed it off.

I was just nervous about seeing Dean tonight. That was it. There was no need to assume something bad was around every corner.

Try not to be a total freak for once, Krista.

I took the stairs down quickly, seeing no one. The cleanup crew must be in a different part of the stadium. As I got to the lower level, I realized I was completely alone.

This wasn't where I was supposed to meet Dean, was it? I checked my phone. He'd said the front entrance. That was all the way around on the other side. I started walking fast, the feeling that I was being stalked only increasing.

I was practically running when I saw them.

"Hey sexy."

I stopped, realizing I had been running towards danger. Not away.

A group of guys stepped out of the shadows and into my path. They had beers. One of them chucked his empty on the ground, the noise jarring me.

"You looking for me sweetheart?"

"No— I'm— meeting my boyfriend."

"Too bad for him we found you first."

"I have to go—"

I tried to brush past them but they blocked my way. I shook my head in fear, stepping back and away.

"Nuh uh uh. I think you should party with us. Do you like to party, cutie?"

They got closer, until I was backed against the wall.

An overhead light blew, the enormous bulb sending glass and sparks raining down on us.

I could barely think. I could maybe have defended myself against one assailant, but this many? I was screwed.

I closed my eyes and screamed. But inside my mind. I tried to reach him.

Dean! Help me!

CHAPTER 33

DEAN

D_{ean}

My blood was pumping, even more than it had during the game. The game I'd crushed, making my debut as starting quarterback more than memorable.

It was freaking *epic*.

But that was just the icing on the cake.

The main event was after the game. When I got to see my sweet girl. Tasty, young, tender Krista. I was going to see her now.

I was going to *claim her.*

I shook my head. I didn't know when I had started thinking about Krista as mine, but the feeling of possessiveness was overwhelming.

I knew I was thinking in archaic terms.

Like a knight. Or a caveman. Yeah that was it. I was turning into a full-blown Neanderthal.

No. Not even that advanced.

I was thinking like an animal.

Basically, I wanted to throw her up in a tower and piss in a circle around her. Then I would challenge anyone who came near her. I'd do more than that.

I would tear their freaking heads off.

That wasn't a normal way to feel about your girlfriend, was it?

And that's what she was. My girlfriend. Starting right now.

I'd tell her as soon as I saw her. I picked up the pace, jogging towards the front entrance of the stadium. It was quiet now, but I'd made sure she wouldn't be standing there alone for long.

I checked my phone again. Krista hadn't written me back but I knew she'd be waiting, exactly where I told her to. I could feel her nearby, sense her presence. I could practically smell her.

That's when I heard it.

I felt it.

Krista was in danger. She needed me. Her fear was palpable.

Dean! Help me!

My head jerked up and I started running. Suddenly I could hear what was happening. The voices were far off, nearly halfway around the stadium from the players exit. But it sounded as if it were happening right beside me.

"Where do you think you're going, cutie?"

I roared, running even faster. I scanned the darkened exterior of the stadium as I blazed ahead, knocking over a trash can as I took a corner.

There, I could see it. About a hundred feet away there was a small crowd. Guys in a semi-circle. Staring at something.

Krista.

I knew it.

I ran faster than I had ever run in my life.

I could see the fear radiating off of Krista, even from far away. She had her shoulders hunched forward and her back pressed up against the wall. There were seven or eight guys surrounding her. They were older. Not students. Local football fans. One of them reached out and touched her shoulder.

"Come on cutie, don't be shy."

The guy was wearing a red shirt.

Then I was there.

Without even breaking stride, my feet left the ground. A split second later my fist connected with the back of the guy's head. All of the power and momentum I'd built up went into that punch. I hit the wall behind Krista and stopped, spinning around.

Red shirt down.

Krista's eyes widened as I stepped in front of her. But I didn't stop to talk. I couldn't do anything but follow my instincts.

Protect. Hurt. Maim.

"Leave her alone. She's mine."

Red shirt was moaning and holding his head but blue shirt and striped shirt cracked their knuckles.

"Yeah, says who?"

"Says freaking me."

Blue shirt drew back to throw a punch. To me it all looked slow motion. I was on the guy before he even started to swing, crushing his fist with one hand. A pathetic scream was the only sound as the guy crumpled, clutching his hand in agony.

Blue shirt down.

"I said leave her the hell alone."

I didn't recognize the voice that was coming out of my mouth. It was lower, more guttural. If I hadn't felt the rumble in my own chest, I would have thought it was someone else speaking.

But it was me. I was the monster now. And I was going to make them pay for touching what was mine.

I grabbed striped shirt and threw him across the causeway. He hit the ground and lay there, unmoving.

Striped shirt down.

"Hey man, that's Dean Westen."

"Let's get the hell out of here."

They took off at a run, the injured limping behind them.

"You'll regret this man!"

I growled, fighting the urge to finish them off. I turned to face Krista. She was breathing fast as she stared into my eyes.

I grabbed her shoulders and turned her into the light, inspecting her for injuries. Relief flooded my body as I realized she was unharmed.

My girl was okay. She was scared, but okay.

But something else was mixed with my relief. I was still angry. I still wanted to kill. But seeing her beauty up close like this was doing other things to me.

I growled and yanked her against me for a kiss.

CHAPTER 34

KRISTA

His *eyes were gold.*

I held my breath as Dean grabbed me and pulled me against him. This was not the same boy I'd met at the beginning of the semester. This was not the boy from my dreams.

This Dean was wild and untamed. He could have killed those men without breaking a sweat. And now he was focused on me.

But I wasn't afraid.

No, in that breathless moment that we stared at each other, I was not afraid at all. I felt myself opening up, accepting him.

All of him. The sweet and the rough. The polite and the untamed. Everything.

His lips came crashing down on mine a moment later.

My mouth opened in surprise. This was different from the other kisses we'd shared, in the dream and in real life. He wasn't just kissing me, he was *kissing me.*

It was epic. A kiss from the old movies. I could practically hear waves crash on the beach.

Yeah, except there was no beach.

My feet dangled helplessly as I struggled for breath, for equilibrium. But not against him. Never against him.

The ground could have been the sky for all I knew. The world felt upside down.

My skin tingled where he touched it. His body giving off waves of heat and I absorbed it all, taking it in. It felt like there was a pool of hot lava rolling around in my belly.

I felt so alive. My senses were suddenly heightened. I wanted him to keep kissing me at the same time that I wanted him to stop, to slow down.

Just a little. Just enough for the world to stop spinning.

I didn't even know what I wanted, or how to put it into words. I was probably in love with Dean. I knew that.

But…

It was happening too fast.

Too fast!

I wrenched away from him, breathing hard as we stared at each other. He could have held me easily but he didn't. He let me go, his breath as labored as mine.

I flinched at the heat in those strange golden eyes of his.

"What is it Krista? Don't tell me you don't want me to kiss you."

I shook my head, trying to get my bearings.

"I won't. I mean, I do."

"Come here then."

He growled and reached for me again. He really did sound like an animal. But one I wanted to pet, not one I was afraid of.

"Just… can we slow down please?"

He didn't move. I could feel his control, his power. He was just waiting to unleash it. I stepped closer, touching my fingertips to his face.

"Dean… what's happening to you?"

His eyes pierced me, filled with torment.

"*You* did this to me."

"What? What did I do?"

"You changed me. And now you are going to make me better."

"I don't understand Dean… What do you mean? How can I make you better?"

He smiled at me. It was not a nice smile.

"I don't know. But being close to you— it helps."

"It— what?"

"I want you with me. *All the time.*"

My eyes widened as he picked me up and threw me over his shoulder. I stopped the scream in my throat. I knew Dean wouldn't hurt me.

But he was freaking me out all the same. I wanted to be with him. I just didn't like being manhandled.

"Where are you taking me?"

"Somewhere we can be alone."

I was upside down for real now, the world turned over. Dean ran, but he barely jostled me. It was uncanny. His control was so great.

I held on tight, the ground was moving fast beneath his feet.

I had no idea where he was taking me. Or why. So I did the only thing I could do. I held onto his shoulders for dear life. I didn't need to though. His grip on me was strong but gentle. I knew without a doubt that he would not drop me.

It was kind of like an amusement park ride.

The trouble was, I hated roller coasters.

I didn't really appreciate being treated like a sack of potatoes and told him so. He growled again. That's when I felt it.

His hands were covered in fur.

My vision was limited to the pavement of the walkway, then the asphalt of the stadium parking lot, then grass, and then the leaves and brush of the woods of the nature preserve behind campus.

I banged on his back to get his attention. He growled again and shifted me. Now, he carried me in front of his body.

It happened so fast I barely had time to blink. I wrapped my arms around his neck, closing my eyes as he ran so fast through the trees that it felt like we were flying.

Finally, he stopped.

It felt like we'd been running forever even though I knew it had been less than an hour. We were deep in the woods with no lights nearby. Nobody could hear what we had to say all the way out here.

The thought was both reassuring and frightening.

He slid me down his body until my feet touched the ground. Dean's breath was ragged. He ducked his head, kissing my neck roughly.

I felt his teeth against my skin. They felt…big.

Really big.

The next thing I knew the ground had risen up to meet my back. Dean had carefully lowered me down. I looked up at him as he bent his head to kiss me again, staring at me with that same hungry, animalistic gaze.

But that wasn't what had my attention.

There was something else happening to him as well… his muscles seemed to ripple in the moonlight. To grow. The hair on his arms was darkening.

I blinked, having trouble believing my eyes.

Was this really happening?

And then his lips crashed down on mine. I gasped at the raw power of the kiss. I knew he wanted more, even though I didn't know exactly what he expected from me.

Of course, he didn't know I was a virgin, did he? He probably had dated lots of girls. But I was… well this was my third kiss, if you wanted to get technical about it.

"Dean, I'm a virgin."

My soft words cut through the night like a blade.

His head snapped up and he stared at me, his eyes seeming to glow in the darkness.

"What?"

"I—I've never done this before. Any of it."

He cursed and let out a howl. My blood turned to ice as I got a good look at him in the moonlight. His head was lifted to the sky. As I watched, his muzzle thickened and elongated.

His teeth glinted white in the darkness. I screamed as he looked at me again, and lowered his head to my throat.

Dean was gone. A monster had taken his place.

SNEAK PEEK OF VAMPIRE PRINCESS

BY CAMERON DRAKE

VAMPIRE PRINCESS

"Behave yourself, Princess."

I rolled my eyes, pulling my backpack over my shoulder. It was new black canvas. I'd had a similar one almost every single school year.

Unfortunately, the last time we'd moved we had been in a hurry, and it had been left behind, along with most of my clothes. I sighed, remembering the sight of our house burning to the ground.

It was to cover our tracks, I knew. Clothes and possessions didn't matter. Only our lives did.

Still, it sucked. I was a girl and I got attached to my stuff. I sighed, shaking it off. At least we had each other. My guardian sat in the car, giving me a look of fond exasperation.

Caleb was strict about my wardrobe. And how I wore my hair. And interacted with other students.

Or rather, how I *didn't*.

It was the same at every new school. Dark colors, plain clothes, no direct eye contact. It was far too dangerous. Not just for me, either.

Caleb, like my father, preached the sanctity of human life. Drink, but don't kill. Glamour, don't destroy. Take but don't harm.

My guardian stared at me, still expecting an answer. He was a worrier. The vamp loved to worry.

I pushed my dark sunglasses up the bridge of my nose and smirked.

"Don't I always?"

He shook his head, remaining in the dark safety of the car. The windows were tinted and he wore gloves and a brimmed hat. It still didn't completely protect him from daylight.

Caleb wasn't like me.

The sun would burn him. Not 'burst into flames and turn to dust' like in the movies, but it wouldn't be pleasant. He'd get singed, like a really bad sunburn. His body would grow weaker, taking days and copious amounts of blood to recover. If he was exposed for long enough, it would kill him.

Or, rather, undo the curse that kept him above ground.

You couldn't technically kill the undead.

Yeah, Caleb was a Vampire. Old school. Like, really old. He'd been one of my father's most trusted advisors. A warrior and a friend.

He was the one who had gotten me out the night they attacked, threw my father in a dungeon, and supposedly killed the young Princess in the process.

Me.

Yep. Yours truly was toast as far as the supernatural world was concerned.

At least that was the rumor.

The new leaders had slaughtered an innocent girl, just to seize power. I wasn't supposed to think their names, let alone say them. As if that could conjure them up. Not that that stopped me. I smirked.

I wasn't afraid of them.

I was going to win. As soon as I mastered my powers. As soon as we had enough rebels on our side.

I turned towards the school, staring up at the red brick and limestone building. It was old, at least a hundred years. It looked like a lot of other schools I'd attended. But this one was somehow prettier than the rest, in that classically institutional way.

I recited the names in my head as I walked towards the big glass doors. It was excellent motivation to keep my eyes on the prize. Maintain my cover. Train as hard as I could.

Survive.

Besides, I was never all that good at following rules. But I liked saying their names while imagining how I would kill them for what they had done. For all the suffering they had caused to so many immortal and human alike.

I'd start with their fingernails. Pull them out one by one. Or their fangs. Or both.

Then I'd move onto the main event, slaughtering them each in turn. Beheading maybe. Or starve them out, then behead them.

I smiled grimly. Yes, slow was definitely better. After all, those bastards were the reason I was in yet another small town registering as a Junior in yet another high school.

Allernon. Jezebel. Dartanian. Bezender.

Yeah, I know. Vampires had really weird names. Especially the old ones. Biblical, Shakespearean names. They sounded silly until you got used to them.

For all I knew, there were vamps somewhere called Danny and Sally, living in the suburbs and buying toilet paper late night at Costco.

But if there were a bunch of true blue American Vampires running around and watching Netflix while drinking the pizza delivery boy, I hadn't met them.

The crazy thing was, I was their leader. Their sovereign by birth. And they might not even know I ever existed.

The four Vampires who had overthrown my father's kingdom had made sure of that. It was forbidden to seven speak my name. My real name, which we never used in public.

Sasha Katherine Uzeliac.

Yeah, I know. It's a mouthful.

I reached for the door just as someone else did. I yanked my hand away, fingers tingling. I didn't like to be touched. Or at least, I wasn't used to it.

Caleb might have saved me, but he wasn't exactly the cuddly type.

Massive blue eyes peered down at me. I blinked, staring up at the cutest boy I'd seen in my life. He smiled and I felt myself melt.

Scratch that. He wasn't cute. Yeah, 'cute' didn't begin to cut it. The guy was freaking gorgeous. GQ, Abercrombie, grown-up Disney star gorgeous.

He gave me a funny look. Probably because I was staring at him, utterly dumbfounded.

"Hey. Are you alright?"

"Uh… yeah. Just trying to, you know, go inside."

He laughed and held the door open for me.

"After you."

For a split second, I was terrified that I had accidentally glamoured him. It happened all the time. I had only to make a wish, or project a thought while maintaining eye contact and any human would pretty much bend over backwards to do what I wanted.

And follow me around like a puppy dog for the rest of their lives.

I'd had to skip town because of it at least a dozen times. It was the most conspicuous thing about me. Other than the whole, unbelievably strong, fast and magically immortal drinking blood once in a while thing.

Other than that, the Vampire rules didn't apply to me. I could go to church. I could go in the sun. I could probably drink a gallon of holy water, though I hadn't tried it.

Ew, gross.

I made a face, imagining drinking tap water that a Priest had dipped his fingers in repeatedly while incanting Latin. Nothing against Priests. But really, you never knew if someone was diligent about washing their hands.

I reached up and touched the hard plastic frame of my dark sunglasses. I exhaled in relief as I walked through the door. There was no way he'd been influenced through these.

The kid was just being polite.

I smiled to myself. Maybe he just liked redheads. I tucked my hair behind my ears, trying to flatten it. It was the one thing I couldn't hide. If the traitors knew anything about me, my hair would be the thing that gave me away.

It was bright pinkish red and couldn't be dyed. One of those weird vamp things. Once you were vamp, you were stuck with your 'do. Even though in my case, it was still growing, getting longer each year. I could trim it but it grew super-fast.

Talk about conspicuous. My head was like a beacon. It was impossible to miss me in a crowd unless I kept it covered up. Basically, I wore a lot of hats.

"You new here?"

I nodded, looking around. There were kids milling around and grabbing books from lockers. It was like every other high school I'd set foot in.

And I'd set foot in a lot. It was always the same. Everyone just going about their business, in a hurry to grow up.

Other than Mr. Wonderful here of course. He didn't seem to be in a hurry to do anything but stare at me.

He grinned. It wasn't the slavish, dazed smile of someone who was under my spell. It was just a guy, being friendly.

Relax Sash.

I reminded myself how to be a normal teenager. Slouch a little. Be nice, but not too nice. Blend.

Just a few more years of this and I would be free. And it wasn't that bad. Not really. I actually liked learning, unlike most of the teenage humans I'd come into contact with.

"Yeah, why?"

"I would have noticed you."

Swoon. Okay, so the guy was definitely a flirt. That was fine. It's not like I was going to start hanging out with mortals, no matter how dreamy they were.

Just blow it off, Sash.

Stay hidden. Stay alive.

I adjusted my bag and pulled my hair over my face. I was going to have to yank the sunnies to go to the admin office, and that meant using my hair as a shield.

"I need to register. Nice meeting you."

He fell in step beside me.

"Dean. Nice to meet you..."

He was dangling for my name. Unfortunately, I couldn't freaking remember what it was this time. Whoops. I ran through the list of names I rotated through, switching it up slightly with each new town and each new school.

Julie... Justine... Celeste... Sophie...

"Sophie."

I hoped that was the freaking name on my documents this time anyway. 'S' names were the easiest to use since they were the closet to my real name. I was getting sloppy. I hadn't bothered to check the paperwork Caleb had stuffed in my bag this morning.

"That's pretty."

"Uh huh."

Jeez, could the guy not take a hint? I turned away, not caring if I seemed rude. Maybe I *had* glamoured him. I knew it could happen from our scent alone sometimes. It was meant to calm those around us.

It helped to make sure they didn't freak out when we started drinking them like a glass of OJ.

This guy was not calm either though. Not exactly. He was sticking to me like glue. I jumped as he grabbed my shoulder. His smile only got wider when I glared at him. He jerked his head in the opposite direction.

"The admin office is that way."

Then he strolled off, whistling.

Whistling! Almost like he'd known what I was thinking. I scowled at his broad back for a split second. He turned and caught me staring. And then he winked.

Ugh, don't encourage him Sash.

I hastened down the rapidly emptying hallway towards the admin office. It went relatively quickly. My documents were fake, but they were forged by an eleven-hundred -year-old Vampire.

In other words, they were flawless.

Caleb was pretty much like Tesla and Einstein rolled into one. He'd been born with a big brain. Plus, he'd had a heck of a lot longer to learn and study.

The man read books so fast and so often it was astounding. And he never got bored. He just loved learning. It was a love he'd passed on to me, though I was nowhere near as fast.

Caleb was brilliant and could do just about anything.

Anything except make a joke. The man was utterly humorless. Thank goodness for Bernard. He was a lot younger, as far as my father's inner circle went. About four hundred years old.

Bernard was… not the sharpest tool in the shed in comparison. Not a dummy by any means, but not a scholar either. Not that it made me love him any less.

He was the affectionate one in our trio. He was sweet and loved to laugh. And he was incredibly big and strong, even for a Vampire. I adored them both equally.

Of course, he wasn't big on hugging his future queen either. Future queen IF I even survived to my eighteenth birthday and reached my full powers. And that was a pretty big 'if.' I had over a year to go.

And I still had a lot to learn in my training.

"Homeroom is down this way. And here is the combination for your locker."

I glanced at the paper for a split second before crumpling it up. Yeah, a photographic memory was one of the many unfair advantages I had over my human classmates. Never growing old being the main one, of course.

At least, I thought I wouldn't grow old. I was aging somewhat normally for a human, but that had begun to slow down. Caleb had a theory that once I finished puberty, I'd stop changing and become like them.

Frozen in time.

The administrator opened the door and waved the teacher over. Mr. Jones was a quiet, thoughtful seeming man. He looked a bit overwhelmed and waved me to a seat without any fuss.

I tried to ignore the stares from my classmates, tugging my hair over my eyes. It was my first day and I was determined to make it here for a couple of months at least. We'd moved in over the weekend and I liked the new house.

It was… homey.

My guardians had provided for me over the years. They gave me everything I could possibly need to grow and survive. But the one thing we'd never had in all these years was a real home.

We were running too much for that.

"Class this is Sophie Wallace. Make her welcome."

I felt every single person in the room look at me and then away. Good. I was doing my best to repel them, which worked most of the time. Sort of an anti —glamour. I could push people away as well as attract them.

Most of the time anyway.

It helped me attract as little attention as possible. The fact that I was wearing the blandest clothes ever and no makeup didn't hurt either. Most teenage girls made at least a token attempt at being stylish. I did… not. I sighed.

I would have loved to go shopping, believe me.

Half the kids were yawning, clearly wishing they were still in bed. I sat and did my best to look bored. It wasn't much of a stretch.

There were several announcements over the loudspeaker and then a bell rang. Everyone jumped up and left except the girl sitting next to me. She had light brown hair and glasses over her intelligent blue eyes.

"Hi."

She smiled shyly and waited for me to grab my bag. I hid my surprise. Kids here were... friendlier than many of the ones I'd encountered.

"Hey."

"I'm Karen. Do you need help finding your way to first period?"

I nodded. I had no clue which way next period was. Being rude was pointless and anyway, the girl seemed nice. It was too bad Caleb had forbidden me from making friends.

I wasn't allowed human friends anyway.

He might be okay if I found a damn wood sprite to chill with. Or a vamp or two. I'd only met a handful of other supernaturals, and those were the ones Caleb had known for centuries.

"Can I see your schedule?"

I made a show of pulling it out to show to her. I'd memorized it instantly of course, but there was no way she could know that.

"Yeah, here."

"Oh, we have two classes together! English lit and bio!"

I nodded, slipping my sunglasses back into place for the stroll through the hallways. I knew it made me conspicuous but it was worth it to keep people from falling at my feet.

Caleb said it gave me a big head.

Personally, I did not enjoy the whole mindless worship routine, but it did come in handy when we were on the run or needed to disappear from a human's memory. I definitely didn't need to use it on an unsuspecting high school kid.

"You have advanced Calc 2 first. Wow, that's a senior AP class."

I shrugged. I didn't want to brag. Besides even the AP classes were going to be dull for me. Caleb had been feeding me all kinds of academic books for years. And since I didn't need to sleep much, well, I read all night. Pretty much every night.

It's not like I had anything else to do. Train. Read. Blend. Read some more.

I even lugged around piles of books when we were on the run. Hopefully that wouldn't happen again for a while. I craved stability at this point. And I was tired. Not physically of course. But mentally, I was tapped out.

We all were.

"Come on, slowpoke."

Karen hurried down the hall, not waiting for me to catch up. Good. I didn't need to be coddled. I allowed myself a small smile.

I liked this chick already.

I glanced over my shoulder and frowned. I turned back to the front of the classroom, biting my lip in worry.

Yep. He was still staring. Mr. Blue Eyes was in my first class.

Fantastic.

I sighed heavily, feeling his eyes on my back. The next time I looked back though, he was talking to the guy sitting next to him under his breath.

Good. Weird, but good. If I had glamoured him accidentally he would be focused on me almost exclusively. So he wasn't glamoured.

He was just... I risked a peek back. Yeah. He was looking at me again. He caught my eye and smiled. I exhaled through my teeth, packing up my books. Not surprisingly, pre —calc was going to be a waste of time for me.

Just like the rest of the classes. I imagined college would be a little more interesting, but maybe not by much.

I sighed. I needed to attend class to appear normal. At least literature and history were somewhat interesting, if only because it was subjective. I liked hearing the different opinions people had on what the great writers and figures in human history had been thinking.

Mostly because it made me laugh. The way people thought was so limiting. Not every author had some higher purpose to teach future generations. A lot of the meaning for them was in the act of writing and sharing their thoughts. They had cherished the act of examining the beauty in the smallness of human life, not trying to make Nand, sweeping statements about the meaning of life. And since Caleb had known some of those great writers in person, I knew a wee bit more than I should about them.

I went to my locker and put my books away, already bored to tears. *Suck it up, buttercup.* A random teenage runaway was much more conspicuous than a shy girl attending classes.

In truth, I was far from shy. And I sucked at keeping my mouth shut. But I had to. Our lives depended on it.

After all, a high school in rural North Carolina was the last place the New Leaders would be looking for me. Yes, that's what the traitors called themselves. And as ridiculous as it sounded, the name had stuck.

I snickered to myself every time I thought about it. It sounded like a 90s boy band. I could almost imagine them, four ancient Vampires in shiny black leather, singing and dancing in unison while teenage girls screamed.

I couldn't wait to tell them that. Just before I tore their heads off and saved my father. I'd even come up with fake song titles and bad lyrics for them.

I'm a cheesy Vampire, baby
Let me suck you up
I might be cold, but I'm hot for you
Boop bop beep oooo

Yeah, I could go on forever. I was very easily entertained. It was a good thing too, considering all I did in my spare time was train.

"Hey. Are you a Senior?"

I shook my head. The bell had barely rung and Mr. Blue Eyes was there, standing at my side. He was almost as sneaky as a freaking vamp!

"No, I'm a Junior."

"Wow, you must be really smart."

I raised my eyebrows, forgetting to hide my eyes.

"I guess."

I *was* freaking smart dammit. But being an honor student was just part of my cover. Maybe I should tone it down a bit… get a B or something.

But that would make Caleb lose his damn mind. I almost smiled, imagining him trying to ground me. *Princesses do not get B's.*

"Wow, your eyes…"

I flinched. I did not want him staring into my eyes. Ugh. I realized I must have forgotten my color contacts. They muted the unusual color and seemed to help with the accidental hypnotism as well.

"What about them?"

My voice sounded a little sharp, but I couldn't help it. My eyes were the one visibly weird thing about me. They were not in the normal range of human eye colors and I was self —conscious about them.

I hated them, to be honest. I said they were like rat eyes, though Caleb told me they looked like Liz Taylor's. He said that they were beautiful.

He even made me watch some old movies to prove it.

"They are sort of purple. No, they're violet."

I shrugged and grabbed my stuff. This kid was making me nervous now. He'd stared directly into my bare eyes and what — not even a hint of mindless adoration?

I must be losing my touch.

"Yeah, I guess it's a genetic mutation or something. It's worse under fluorescent lights."

He smiled and I felt the tension go out of my body. I'd expected a comment about rodents or fake contacts. If only he knew how unusual my eyes really were…

"They're nice."

I watched him walk away, staring after his broad back and long legs. Nice? My eyes were nice?

That was… the most ordinary compliment I'd ever gotten.

"Miss Wallace?"

I realized I was standing in the middle of the empty classroom. I shook myself and hurried to my next class.

Yeah, being back in high school was a boatload of freaking fun.

TURN THE PAGE FOR AN EXCERPT OF
DREAMSHIFTERS BOOK TWO AND SECOND
SIGHT FROM KARA SEVDA

MOON BOUND

DEAN

"Stay away from me."

My eyes fluttered open. I was laying on the ground. Above me faint light filtered through the trees. It was early in the morning from the looks of it. And it was freezing.

"What the—"

"I said stay away from me!"

I turned my head to see Krista kneeling on the ground with a long stick pointed at me. Right at my chest.

A very *sharp* stick.

Her big brown eyes were wide with fear. Her back was pressed up against a tree trunk. She looked like she was shivering.

From the cold or fear, I wasn't sure which.

"Krista?"

"Don't!"

I ran my hand through my hair and brushed the leaves away. I grimaced, expecting to be stiff after sleeping on the ground all night.

Instead I felt good. Really good.

In fact, I felt fantastic.

"What the hell happened?"

She whimpered and waved the stick menacingly. I almost laughed. She was about as threatening as a kitten. I grabbed the stick and tossed it away playfully.

That's when I noticed her eyes were filling up with tears.

"Hey… it's okay Krista. I'm not going to hurt you."

She scrambled away and was on her feet in an instant. I reached out and grabbed her just as she started to run. It was like taking candy from a baby.

I could tell that she was frightened of something. I wanted to tell her not to be scared. That I would protect her.

Always.

But I had a terrible feeling that the something she was afraid of was *me*.

"Krista, what's wrong? Did something happen to you?"

She stared up at me, the look in her eyes nearly breaking my heart.

"You carried me away… and then you…"

I reached out for her and pulled her into my arms. She stood stiffly, not relaxing into me like she had every other time she'd been in my arms. My eyes narrowed in frustration.

This could not be happening. My sweet girl could not be afraid of me. I would never do something to spook her away.

Except… I couldn't exactly remember how I'd gotten there. Or what had happened the night before…

"No way. I didn't hurt you. I wouldn't."

"You didn't hurt me, but…"

"But what?"

I stroked her hair back from her face tenderly. I pulled a leaf out of her tangled waves and smiled. Her huge eyes were shining. She had a smudge of dirk on her cheek. But she still looked beautiful.

"You can tell me. It's alright."

"I just want to go home now, please."

"Krista, please tell me what happened. I can't… remember anything after the game."

She looked at me searchingly. She wanted to believe me, I could tell. So why didn't she? I'd never lied to her before. I wouldn't. I wasn't sure I even could.

I could feel her wavering between fear and compassion.

"You really can't?"

I shook my head and tried to smile reassuringly. Some of the tension went out of her shoulders.

"Okay. I'll tell you. But later, okay?"

I nodded. I would give her time. On one condition.

"Alright Krista, you win. Just one last thing..."

I saw her startled eyes register that I was about to kiss her a split-second before I did. My lips found hers. She stiffened up, feeling like a board in my arms. She relaxed as I kissed her softly. There was no urgency or pressure, just... us.

It was a long time before I lifted my head again. Her eyes were trusting now. I followed her as she turned and walked out of the forest, all without saying a word.

What the hell had happened last night?

SECOND SIGHT

He almost caught her. Almost. His hands nearly caught on the soft cotton of her white blouse. But she disappeared in the flutter of falling apple blossoms. Behind a tree. And then another. Twisting and turning through the orchard.

Gone.

"Lisetta!" He whispered her name harshly. He was growing nervous, afraid. He didn't want to miss a moment of this. Their long awaited secret meeting. It had been weeks since he last saw her face, held her, touched her.

Today he had something important to tell her.

Hands closed over his eyes suddenly, making him jump in fear. But the hands were delicate, soft. They followed him as he tried to spin around. A girlish giggle warmed his ear. A sweet, familiar scent washed over him.

"Pietro..." She caressed his neck teasingly before releasing him. He turned around, reaching for her. This time he caught her easily. She was ready to be caught.

He looked down at her. His beautiful girl. His forbidden girl. Her dark hair curling around her jaw, the gentle curve of her cheek. She stared at him with her large brown eyes. She reminded him of a doe, something wild, but temporarily tamed.

Pietro watched her carefully as he lowered himself onto his knee. He held her hand tightly, certain she would bolt.

The mischievous look in her eyes was replaced by astonishment as he pulled something out of his pocket. A ring. One his father had given to him when he became a man.

He looked up at her, his handsome face solemn. They were not supposed to be there in the orchard. They were not supposed to venture to this hill, overlooking his home and hers. They were supposed to be enemies, not lovers. But they had been drawn to each other from the start, from the first time he had seen her sweet little face in the square. Before his mother yanked him away. Before her father drew the hood of her cape down. He had seen her. She had seen him. And they had known.

PRESENT DAY

Professor Weilright sat behind his desk, looking over the folder. Not just any folder. This was *her* folder. It was overstuffed with papers and notes and God knows what. Lizzy could see red writing here and there, making corrections, comments, leaving a final unsatisfactory mark. God knows there had been enough of those this year.

She shifted in her chair impatiently. A slim girl with long golden brown hair, she was prettier than she thought she was. But even if she knew, she wouldn't have cared.

She rolled her eyes, sighing heavily. How long was this going to take? She knew what he was going to say to her anyway. She didn't really need an encore of what she'd heard from three other teachers already.

Her fingers drummed the armrest of the stiff backed chair. The sound must have been kind of annoying because

Professor Weilright stared at her pointedly. Lizzy stopped drumming.

The office was dim, a bit dusty, but comfortable. She wondered idly the last time Professor Weilright had straightened up. The leaded glass windows didn't let in much light, but maybe the was a good thing.

The Forsythe academy was ancient. The ultra exclusive prep school had been in existence for two hundred and thirty seven years, and the formerly private estate it resided in, at least one hundred more. Some of the girls complained about the drafts and creaky floorboards but secretly Lizzie liked it.

It reminded her of the Museums she had visited as a child with her mother. It was… substantial. There wasn't much she liked about being sent away to boarding school but there was that.

She liked old shit. It was a good thing too, all things considered.

Professor Weilright exhaled and leaned back in his chair. She looked up sharply, sensing that the moment was at hand. Here we go.

"Elizabeth-"

"Lizzy."

"Lizzy. You are a smart girl."

"Thank you."

"You are a very smart girl who is either purposefully failing or is obviously suffering from…"

She looked at him expectantly. This ought to be good. Lizzy leaned forward in her seat as he peppered her with rapid fire questions.

"Drug addiction?"

"No."

"Eating disorder?"

"Um, no!"

"Teen pregnancy?"

"At an all girls school? That would be impressive, but no."

He held up his hands.

"Okay Lizzy, I tried. We are supposed to ask these questions. But with you I suspect it's more complicated than that. Have you been keeping up your sessions with Dr. Allen?"

"It's a waste of time. Dr. Allen doesn't know his ass from his elbow."

It looked for a moment as if Professor Wcilright agreed with her when he struggled to conceal his smirk. It was too bad she had decided not to try this year. Professor Weilright was smarter than most. His class was almost enjoyable.

Almost.

"Well, be that as it may part of your acceptance at this school was contingent on your... continued therapy sessions."

She looked out the window over his head, at the floor, anywhere but at him. Her mental health (or lack thereof) was by far her least favorite topic of conversation. Of course, adults always wanted to talk about it. They thought they could understand, make sense of it somehow. Solve the puzzle girl and win the prize.

But she knew they couldn't.

"Not to mention you are failing my class. You won't be allowed back for senior year if you can't get a C minus at the very least. And continue with Dr. Allen."

Her fingers started tapping again as she studied the pattern in the faded afghan carpet. It really was a lovely shade of aubergine. Aubergine. That was whale puke, right? Yum.

"Lizzy. Lizzy!"

She took a deep breath and looked back up at him. It was time to face the music. Might as well do it with some dignity.

"You don't want to fail do you?"

She shrugged. Lizzy had learned long ago not to fight city hall. Or her own lack of interest in pleasing the powers that be. Apathy was the safest course. Besides, she'd noticed that adults were more than happy to brush lost causes under the carpet. If she didn't have wealthy parents, or an annoying ability to do well on standardized tests, she wouldn't be at this school to begin with.

"Do you want to be sent home to repeat the eleventh grade in... dare I say... public school?"

"No. I mean, no I don't want to go home." It was true. As much as she resented being shuffled off half way around the world, getting sent back in disgrace would be much worse. Much. Her stepmonster would never shut up about it.

Plus she couldn't leave Al to face the wolves alone.

"But you don't really like it here, do you?"

"It's alright."

He stared at me over his folded hands. 'Alright' wasn't the response you expected when asking about one of the best schools in Europe. But she never lied. It wasn't because she was on some moral high horse.

She was just too lazy.

"So, what are we going to do about this?"

"Pass me anyway?"

Lizzy looked up at him hopefully, doing her best puppy dog eyes. He frowned, not buying it. She sighed. She knew he wouldn't. It was one of the things she liked about him.

She quickly lost respect for people who took things at face value. Especially when sarcasm pretty much leaked out

154

of her bones in this sort of situation. She didn't like confrontation. Lizzy went out of her way to make it as uncomfortable for everyone else around her as well.

"I wouldn't be doing you any favors with a free ticket. No, you are going to do an extra credit make up essay. On which I will base…"

Professor Weilright riffled through his desk for his grade book. He traced his finger down the column marked 'Elizabeth Cutler'. She leaned forward, curiosity getting the better of her. It's was a pathetic line of F's with one D and a B minus. He caught her looking and slammed the book shut.

"One hundred percent of your grade."

He was being overly generous. She knew it. He had been giving her sorrowful looks all semester. If he was trying to make her feel guilty, it had worked. Just not enough for her to start caring again.

The funny thing was, she used to care. Used to sit at her desk until she had completed all her assignments, most of which came almost too easily to her. Lizzy had a brain like a sponge, only having to read something once before knowing it by rote. A couple of years ago her marks were an unbroken line of straight A's. That's how she ended up in a school that catered to the wealthiest families in Europe. Lot of good it had done her.

One day she woke up and just didn't feel like trying anymore.

Lizzy sighed for what felt like the hundredth time. He was trying to help, she knew that much. Besides, what choice did she have?

"What kind of essay?"

"For you I think something juicy... something to get riled up about yes?"

155

That sounded as appealing as whale puke.

"Okay. What?"

"You said you were spending the summer in Italy with your family didn't you?"

She nodded cautiously. He leaned back in his chair, putting his hands behind his head. She could see a devilish twinkle in his eyes.

"That sounds relaxing. Laying by the pool, eating pasta… exploring the state of womens rights during the past few centuries."

She groaned.

Students milled around the courtyard, revealing in the afternoon sun and the promise of summer. The school was perched high in the mountains which meant it never really got warm here. But the sun was shining and soon we would all be gong home.

Or wherever.

Lizzy walked around the periphery, trying to be as unobtrusive as possible. It didn't work.

Heads swiveled to watch her as she walked through. Everyone knew who Lizzy was. Everyone knew just enough of her story to know she'd been in a mental hospital. She didn't care what they thought. She just didn't want certain, specific people bothering her.

Not today.

A group of tall Nordic looking girls caught sight of her as she skirted the crowd. They smirked at each other, snickering as she passed. Fantastic. Lizzy resisted the urge to look down at herself, to see what had set off their mean spirited giggles. Not that she was s sharp dresser by any stretch of the imagination, but she was wearing a damn uniform.

Lizzy almost sagged in relief as a sultry looking blond with cats eyes led the group out of the courtyard Megan was their ringleader and the most popular girl in school. Or at least, the most feared. She had some sort of vendetta against Lizzy for some unknown reason.

Lizzy had a sneaking suspicion that Megan was the one who'd gotten into the school's confidential files and spread the word about her hospitalization.

Lizzy did her best to ignore her. It wasn't easy.

At the far corner of the yard there was a copse of trees and shrubbery. She darted behind them as soon as no one was looking.

Nestled in the greenery was Alberta, a cherubic English girl with mousy brown hair and round glasses. She sat on a decrepit old bench, palming a smoke.

"Oh, it's just you. I thought it was one of the wardens."

Sometimes Alberta liked to pretend the exclusive girls academy was a reform school for wayward girls. Lizzy wasn't even sure they still had reform schools, but it wasn't too far off. It might be one of the best schools in the world academically but the thin wool blankets were straight out of 'Oliver.' Most of the girls brought their own bedding. Lizzy was too proud to ask her dad and stepmother to ship stuff from America, so she was stuck with a couple of extra wool blankets she'd snagged from the housekeeping staff.

Of course, she had to share them with Al. Her Nan was too cheap to send her anything extra. Like Lizzy, Al had lost a parents. Both of them. Lizzy had just lost one, even though it felt like they both disappeared forever that day.

She sat down next to Alberta on the bench, ignoring the dead leaves and moss. Not like you would notice a grass stain on the navy pleated skirts they had to wear.

"How'd it go then?"

Lizzy glared at Al, taking the cigarette and dragging deeply.

"That good, eh?"

She grunted and pulled on the smoke. Lizzy was beyond words. Alberta chuckled. She thought she was funny apparently. It was a good thing she did since they girls had been roommates for the past two years and the best friends in the whole world. Lizzy smiled at her wanly and gave her back her cig.

"Not as bad as I thought."

"Good." Al stood and chucked the cig into a pile of butts under the tree. "Well come on then, we better pack."

ACKNOWLEDGMENTS

Cover: Mayhem Cover Creations
    Image: Depositphotos
    Editing: Red Lily Publishing
    Publishing: Pincushion Press

ABOUT THE AUTHORS

Cameron Drake and Kara Sevda are avid readers of Paranormal Fiction. This is Kara and Cameron's first collaboration together.

The series continues in DreamShifters Book Two: Moon Bound, coming soon!

Follow them on Facebook and Amazon for updates and more:

Cameron Drake's Facebook Page

Cameron Drake's Amazon Page

Kara Sevda's Facebook Page

Kara Sevda's Amazon Page

ALSO BY CAMERON DRAKE

Vampire Princess

COMING SOON

Vampire Princess Book Two

Dreamshifters Book Two: Moon Bound

ALSO BY KARA SEVDA

Second Sight

The Dune Walkers

COMING SOON

Dreamshifters Book Two: Moon Bound

Made in the USA
San Bernardino, CA
20 March 2019